BOOTHILL RIDERS

When Ed Burnett, newspaperman-printer, landed in Box Elder, Montana, he crossed the biggest cattle man in the territory. Gardner stirred up the town for a lynching and killed a man in self-defence, and by the time it was cleared up he had Box Elder's first front page story.

Books by Lee Floren
in the Linford Western Library:

BLACK GUNSMOKE
LOBO VALLEY
DEADLY DRAW
THE SADDLE WOLVES
SHOOT-OUT AT MILK RIVER
RIMROCK RENEGADE
THE HARD RIDERS
RUSTLER'S TRAIL
WOLF DOG RANGE
RIFLE ON THE RANGE
GUN WOLVES OF LOBO BASIN
HIGH BORDER RIDERS
ROPE THE WILD WIND
BROOMTAIL BASIN
PUMA PISTOLEERS
THE GUN LORDS OF STIRRUP BASIN
DOUBLE CROSS RANCH
FOUR TEXANS NORTH
WOLF DOG TOWN
THE LAST GUN
THE LONG TRAIL NORTH
MONTANA MAVERICK
BLOODY RIFLES

LEE FLOREN

BOOTHILL RIDERS

Complete and Unabridged

LINFORD
Leicester

First published in the
United States of America in 1978

First Linford Edition
published November 1990

British Library CIP Data

Floren, Lee, *1910–*
Boothill riders.—Large print ed.—
Linford western library
I. Title
813.52[F]

ISBN 0–7089–6940–2

Published by
F. A. Thorpe (Publishing) Ltd.
Anstey, Leicestershire

Set by Words & Graphics Ltd.
Anstey, Leicestershire
Printed and bound in Great Britain by
T. J. Press (Padstow) Ltd., Padstow, Cornwall

THE driving September rainstorm hit the cowtown of Boxelder, Montana, at noon, smashing down from the Bearpaw Mountains to the south. Then, its first wild fury spent, it settled down to a slow, soil penetrating chilly fall rain.

Water dripping off the eaves of his undertaking parlor had made Mortician Funeral O'Neill sleepy. Now, lanky body angled in his swivel chair, he slept with his boots on his battered desk, head on his chest.

He did not hear the young woman enter. She shook him violently awake, his boots thudding to the splintery wooden floor.

His blue eyes showed surprise.

"Millie Wetherford, what in the name of tarnation is wrong with you? Coming into my office like this and waking me up. Shucks, girl, I was dancing with a pretty can-can girl, I was. And now you've made me lose her!"

"Funeral, I haven't got time to joke." She was panting as though she had been running. "I been looking for you for about ten minutes. First I went to your house, but you weren't there – "

"What do you want, Millie?"

"Oh, Funeral, this is terrible – Ed – Ed Burnett – He's just killed Colt Hagen, Funeral!"

Had there been any vestiges of sleep left in the landy undertaker, the girl's words would have driven them hurriedly away. Funeral let his boots drop to the floor and he leaned forward in the chair, apparently doubting the validity of her words.

"Millie Wetherford, what has gone wrong with you? What are you trying to tell me, girl? Why, Ed Burnett – Ed wouldn't harm – "

Her voice held a touch of hysteria. Tears were in her pretty brown eyes. "Oh, Funeral, it was awful. Colt Hagen – he came into the Tribune's office — he was looking for trouble — "

"Yes?"

"And he found it. They fought — him and Ed — and Ed got shot through the leg. Not bad, though, Doc says. Ed says he was only defending himself, and I know he was only doing that — he wouldn't start a fight. But he's in jail now — and the doctor is working on his leg — "

She sank into a chair, hands over her head and she sobbed. Funeral O'Neill felt pity for her. He got to his feet and crossed his office and slid into his yellow raincoat and got his rain-helmet off the hook. He waited for the girl to stop sobbing. Within a few minutes, she looked up at him. Sanity had her now, making her eyes clear, and she wiped her eyes with a small handkerchief.

"When did all this happen, Millie?"

"About ten minutes ago, I think. I've — lost track of time — I'm so worried about Ed. Like I said, I went first to your house, looking for Funeral. Mr. O'Neill, we have to do something."

"Best thing we can do now," Funeral assured, "is to keep level heads."

She daubed at her eyes and managed to smile. "I love Ed so much," she said. He's' such a fine fellow – such a good man – "

Her head went down again.

Funeral remained standing, a lanky man of about thirty five. He had a long narrow face and his eyes were soft as he watched the girl. He had never married, not so much a bachelor because of choice but because he had never met the right woman. He wondered why he had not heard the shots. Then the answer came: He had been sleeping, the rain made quite a noise, there had been and was some errant thunder occasionally, and evidently the gunfight had taken place inside a building, the Tribune office. Because he thought of the Boxelder Tribune, he thought of young Ed Burnett, its publisher. And, because he thought of young Ed, who was about twenty one or so, he thought of the first time he had met the young man, about two years ago when he, Funeral, had accompanied a trainload of cattle back to the slaughter pens in Omaha, Nebraska, miles to the east.

There he had met a young reporter, not more than nineteen or so, whose beat it was to find feature stories and news items, there in the stockyard area. And this man had stuck out his hand and had said, "I understand you are Mr. O'Neill, sir? An undertaker, called Funeral O'Neill?"

Funeral had looked at the young man, liking his open face and pleasant manner. And his hand had gone out automatically.

"And who are you, sir?"

"The name, Mr. O'Neill, is Ed Burnett. I'm a reporter for the Globe. But that is not what I want to talk to you about. My father, sir, used to mention you often; you and he went to the same mortician school."

Funeral had let his memory sweep back a period of time. He had been out of veterinarian school, at this time, for about thirteen years or so and memory was fickle. But memory could not eliminate Mack Burnett, Funeral's best friend in college. Mack had been about eight years older than he had been, but between them had been a strong friendship. Mack had been a married student and this boy — now a reporter — had then been a small child.

"Well, I'll he hanged," Funeral had said, smiling as he had shaken the youth's hand. "And how is your father, Ed?"

"He's dead."

"Dead?" Funeral had been surprised. He had not received a letter from Mack Burnett for three years but their correspondence had always been spasmodic, so he had thought nothing of the long lapse of time between letters. "Nobody wrote to me, Ed."

"I was in Chicago, working as a printer's devil. I thought my mother had told you, sir."

"How did you know I was coming in

with this load of cattle?"

"Saw your name on the manifest, sir."

"Well, sure good to see you, Ed, and sure sorry to hear about your father. I remember you when you were just a little boy."

"I must have been about four years old, huh?"

"Somewhere along that."

During the few days, Funeral had spent in Omaha, he and Ed Burnett spent most of that time in each other's company. Funeral found him to be a fine young man, open-minded and of good personality. They went to shows together, even attended the burlesque, and they had a few drinks together, although both were not much of a hand at hard liquor.

But Ed had confided in Funeral, and the boy had one burning desire in life, and this desire was to print and own his own newspaper, preferably a country weekly. He was saving his money toward this point from a salary already meager and small, Funeral listened and had his thoughts but he said nothing.

So Funeral had returned to Boxelder. Then came a stroke of luck that was rough on the old publisher of the Boxelder-Tribune but good for young Ed Burnett. For the old editor suffered a stroke and died. Funeral and his partner, Veterinarian Ringbone Smith, had purchased the paper, and then had wired for young Ed Burnett, who came as fast as train could carry him.

Now the undertaker asked, "How bad is Ed hurt, honey?"

"He got shot in the leg when they tussled for Colt Hagen's gun. Ed hit Hagen with that lead mallet he pounds type into place with. That mallet – well, it's heavy, Funeral."

"Bet it sure dented Hagen's thick skull," Funeral said.

The girl's voice was still high pitched. "Clint Gardner is behind this killing, Funeral. I know that, just as sure as I'm a foot tall. Gardner has ordered Hagen over to the Tribune office to kill Ed. Ed has been fighting that dirty Gardner in the Tribune and Gardner has sent Hagen to kill Ed."

Funeral O'Neill had already slid into his oilskin slicker. Now he pulled on his wide rain-helmet.

"We'd best look into this, Millie."

They went outside into a gloomy rain-ruined afternoon. You could not see the clouds because of the mist caused by the rain, but Funeral knew the clouds hung low to the peaks surrounding this Montana cowtown.

Millie hung onto his arm.

Despite the stiffness of his slicker, he could feel the tension of her fingers as they ground into his arm.

"I know Gardner sent Hagen over to kill Ed," she repeated.

Funeral said nothing. He was busy with his thoughts. He was wide awake now. His thoughts went to the cowman named Clint Gardner. Gardner owned the immense Circle S cow-outfit, the biggest spread in these parts. And the farmers were moving in on this range. They were filing on homesteads and running out barbwire fences and building sod shacks and their plows were turning over the virgin soil, breaking the roots of the buffalo-grass. Their fences were turning back Circle S cattle, keeping Gardner cattle from grazing on land which he claimed as grazing areas, although he did not own deeds to this land.

Ed Burnett and his Tribune had backed the case of the farmers. Ed had written editorials advocating the cause of the farmers. These editorials, of course, had not sat well with Cowman Clint Gardner.

Some of the farmers had run into trouble. Their fences had been mysteriously cut, the wires had been dragged down for miles, the posts jerked or broken from the ground. They had lost some cattle and horses to night riders. Ed had tabulated these points in a recent editorial, appealing to the Gardner spread to co-operate with his riders had caused this destruction, had run off these stolen horses and cows.

The day after the printing of the editorial, Gardner had accosted Ed Burnett on the street, and had not the onlookers moved in, there might have been a fight – either with guns or with fists.

Millie's words jerked Funeral back to the present.

"Oh, what if Hagen would have killed Ed?"

"He didn't, honey."

Her voice had found its usual steadiness by now. "I love Ed and Ed loves me. When he gets out of jail – and when he gets well – I'm going to marry him regardless of what he says."

"You sound – determined," Funeral said, and smiled.

"I am serious. Ed has held back because he is saving money so he could buy a house before we get married. But we can live in a rented house, we can. I don't want him killed."

Funeral had no reply to this. They hurried toward the court-house. He was glad the girl was talking. Talking would release her tense nerves. She also had her problems, he realized. She was having trouble at home. This trouble was because she had swung into Ed Burnett's line of thinking and she too advocated the cause of the farmers. Her father owned the Mercantile, the big store. Her father was against the farmers, although they had brought more trade to him; still, he was bull-headed — he liked to argue that cattle, not plows, had built up this area, and that his store, until the last year or so, had been supported by the cattleman and cowpunchers, not by the farmers. Funeral wondered how much of this her father really believed. When more farmers came in, trade would boom in the stores. The more people there are in an area the more goods are sold to them. That, to Funeral, was simple arithmetic; he figured Merchant Wetherford was aware of this, too. He was just straddling the fence.

At this moment, a short heavy-set man of about Funeral's age came out of the rain, and he stopped upon seeing them. He was Funeral O'Neill's partner, Ringbone Smith.

"I was heading for your office, Funeral, to tell you about Ed and Hagen, but I see Millie here has beat me to the chore," the vet said.

"You always have been behind times in your life," Funeral joked.

Ringbone scowled. He had a wide face with a wide nose and he continuously chewed peppermints, be they red or blue or any color. Now he rolled one between his teeth and made a sour face.

"We can't all be smart like you," he told his partner with some sarcasm.

"Come along," Funeral ordered, "and shut up."

When they got to the court-house, which was a brown-stone building, they went to the Sheriffs Office, which was in the annex. Quite a number of people were gathered around the outside of Sheriff Dunlap's office, despite the rain. They wore yellow and black slickers and they were a cold-looking outfit. Funeral quickly identified a few farmers in the group. Evidently they had been in town for supplies when the killing had occurred. They were easy to identify for they stood in a group by themselves, men set apart because of their beliefs and their occupations. Funeral did not like this one bit. He counted six farmers. This group had an air of tension and danger in it and he hoped a few hot words would not turn this into a gangfight, for the townsmen, he figured, favored the Gardner spread, seeing most of them had been or still were connected with the cattle-raising business.

He saw two Gardner men in the crowd, and he figured they would be glad to strike the spark that would start this incident into full blaze.

They climbed the few steps and got on the porch. There a heavy-built cowpuncher held his arm out and stopped them.

Funeral looked down at the thick arm, then let his gaze travel to the pock-marked and bloated face.

"Why the arm out, Williams?"

"Nobody is allowed to enter Dunlap's

office, Funeral."

"Who ordered that. Clint Gardner?"

The derisive tone of Funeral O'Neill's words had made the name Clint Gardner a word of insult. This registered on Williams and made his eyes pull down. Funeral had very little use for Clint Gardner. He had never liked the man and Gardner, he knew, did not like him, but both had never let their dislikes come into open trouble between them – between the two was a veiled animosity and antipathy. Gardner had been on this Boxelder range about three years. He had come in a stranger and had bought the Circle S from its former owner and founder, an old man who had then gone to Arizona to get milder climate for his few remaining days. When Gardner had bought the spread it had not run as many head as it now did, nor had it been arrogant and tough – its riders had not stalked down Boxelder's plank sidewalks, half drunk and insulting, pistols tied down on their hips. Nor had the old Circle

S cowpunchers insulted housewives and caused gunfights and death.

"No, not Clint Gardner's orders, undertaker," Williams said, and his voice was surly. "Them is the orders of Sheriff Dunlap. Now step back, you three, and be nice people."

Funeral said, "You seem to forget one thing, Williams."

The frog-like eyes watched him. The thick lips moved slowly. "And what has Williams forgot, undertaker?"

"I'm county coroner. I have a legal right to enter this building. My duty requires I go inside."

"You'll stay outside, and what is more – you'll like it, O'Neill!"

Williams said no more. The undertaker's bony fist pushed the man, driving him back. It was not a blow; it was a push against William's chest. William's pocked face grew blustery, anger narrowed his eyes – and he hit with a vicious right hook.

But the hook only spent itself on the rain-filled air. Williams moved ahead and this time he walked into the undertaker's rising right fist. This was no pushing motion; this was a direct hit.

Funeral's knuckles came in under the man's blocky chin. Williams sat down with a stupid look on his ugly face. Apparently he had never before in his life been knocked down with one blow and the look held as much surprise as it did pain. Funeral almost smiled openly. Ringbone Smith had a dead pan face, only his jaw working as he masticated a peppermint.

"You asked for that," Millie said.

Funeral asked, "I reckon we can go in now, folks."

They went into the long hall. Ringbone Smith looked at his lanky partner. "Never knowed you could belt a man so hard," he said in admiration. "Don't never hit me like that, huh?"

"I'd hit you harder," Funeral joked.

"Williams he won't forget that," the vet warned.

"Then, if he won't forget, he'll have to remember. Well, here we are, at the door to Dunlap's office."

They went into the office. Sheriff Dunlap, a tall and homely man, sat in his chair, long legs out in front of him. Clint Gardner sat across the room and looked up as they entered. He was about thirty, maybe a few years under that mark, and his face was marked by hard lines, for greed and passion pushed him with hard spurs, adding maturity to his face. He looked at them and nodded but said nothing. Sheriff Dunlap said not a word, either: he also merely nodded. Then Funeral went to his knees beside the man who lay on the floor. He knew the man was dead – so he had been told – but his job of county coroner demanded he make a pretense of going through a physical examination of the corpse. So he laid his hand flatly on the man's chest, and there was silence.

"No heart beat," he said, getting to his feet. "Dead."

They all looked down at dead Colt Hagen. Once Hagen owned a reputation as a tough man, a gun toting killer. But Ed Burnett's heavy lead mallet had pounded that reputation out of the man and made him a corpse in the process. Secretly Funeral was happy that the range had been made rid of a dangerous killer.

Clint Gardner's voice had rough edges as it broke the silence. "This ain't the end of this, people!"

Funeral looked at the man. "No," he said, "this hasn't ended, Gardner. You see, there has to be an inquest — a coroner's inquest. We'll hold that tomorrow, Gardner."

Gardner watched him, and tension held the group.

"And at that inquest," Funeral said slowly, "we might wash out some dirty linen."

"Like what, for instance?" Gardner still spoke roughly.

Funeral O'Neill merely shrugged. The harshness of the cowman's voice rubbed against him and drew a touch of anger to him. He glanced at his partner who was chewing that perennial peppermint. His glance met that of Millie Wetherford, but she said nothing. Evidently he had been appointed spokesman, whether he liked it or not.

"Wait until the inquest, Gardner," he murmured.

Gardner's voice drops a degree. "This printer killed one of my top hands. A good man with a horse, a rope, and a saddle. He was foully murdered by a lead mallet. He had dropped in to merely pay up a subscription to the Tribune. And the printer deliberately picked a fight with him and murdered him." Gardner was lying and they all knew it but nobody spoke. "So I hereby charge Ed Burnett with first degree murder, and I want the Sheriff to so issue a warrant."

Sheriff Dunlap looked toward Funeral O'Neill. He had a sort of dumb look on his long face. Funeral knew that Clint Gardner was more forceful than was the sheriff, and he knew, also, that the sheriff was mutely appealing to him, also a county employee, to make a decision, even though that decision belonged, by all rights, to the sheriff to reach.

Funeral had a moment of deviltry. Sheriff Dunlap was in misery, and he decided to add to that misery.

"That is for the sheriff to decide," the undertaker said.

Gardner swung his baleful gaze over to Sheriff Dunlap. By this time Dunlap had gathered his wits somewhat and had found his out. Funeral was somewhat surprised by the man's answer for Dunlap, in Funeral's opinion, had really performed some fast thinking.

"I can't issue the warrant now, Gardner."

"Why not, sheriff?"

"The coroner-jury ain't done met yet," the lawman pointed out. "When it meets, it renders a verdict — if the verdict calls that I issue a warrant for Ed Burnett's arrest, then I issue it. The warrant's severity has to be determined by the verdict of the coroner's jury. If they calls it first-degree murder; the warrant will read first-degree – but if they call it something else, so it will read. And if they call it self defense, I have to free Burnett."

Gardner knew he was beaten, and for a moment his face showed this. "But you have to keep him in jail until the jury returns its verdict," he quickly pointed out.

Dunlap nodded. "Correct ye are, friend."

Gardner switched his gaze to Funeral O'Neill. He was seething inside and Funeral, knowing the nature of this man, was aware of this fact, and he waited for the cowman to speak, knowing full well what the man would say. And the words of Clint Gardner were those he had expected.

"I could get the sheriff to swear out a warrant for your arrest, undertaker."

Funeral thought, he wants trouble. Ringbone Smith had stopped chewing his peppermint. The mint lay unnoticed on his broad tongue. Funeral read this as a danger sign. His veterinarian friend, he knew, was getting angry — Ringbone was slow to move to anger, but once he started moving there would be trouble aplenty. Funeral knew all the signs.

The undertaker spoke slowly. "Seems to me, Gardner, you kind of have the duties of the county officers mixed up in your mind, friend."

"In what way?"

"The sheriff does not *issue* a warrant for a man's arrest. The sheriff merely *serves* the warrant. The warrant is issued by the county judge."

"Don't worry about the legal angles," the cowman said, and his voice held hard edges.

"What would be the grounds for this warrant?"

"Assault and battery upon the person of Williams. You knocked him down, remember? You assaulted him."

Funeral O'Neill gave a deep sigh, feigning relief. "Man, you had me scared for a spell, Gardner. I thought you had a serious charge against me and I was thinking back hell-for-leather to try to remember what I had done wrong. And it does seem to me that Williams hit at me first."

"After you pushed him, yes."

Funeral said, "Let's forget this childish talk, Gardner, about who pushed who, and for why."

Clint Gardner said nothing. Anger was scrawled across his wide face, giving him a look of harshness, making his cheek bones stand out. Funeral looked at Sheriff Dunlap whose long face held a look of misery. Dunlap was plainly wading out beyond his depth. Just then Ringbone Smith turned suddenly and Funeral, turning also, saw Williams go down for the second time within a few minutes. The man lay on the floor, spitting blood.

"He tried to come in behind you," Ringbone Smith said, rubbing the knuckles on his right hand. "I kinda knocked a knuckle back a little, but I've had trouble with that same knuckle before . . . every time I have had to hit something or somebody. Williams, you're a bad boy."

Williams climbed to his feet. He sleeved his mouth and looked at the blood and then looked at Clint Gardner, who nodded his head angrily. Williams let anger flush his face, and then he walked over and sat down on a chair next to the wall, and he glared at Ringbone Smith.

"You had me figured out wrong," he muttered, spitting again.

"In what way?" Ringbone asked.

"I never meant no harm for your partner. I was merely comin' into the room peaceful-like."

Ringbone Smith snorted like a bronc smelling a wolf. "Sure, on tiptoe – so nobody would hear you, and with fists doubled. Jes' a friendly little call, eh?"

Williams looked at him. Then he looked at Clint Gardner.

Momentarily rebellion ran across William's eyes. But he got to his feet and shuffled out, not glancing back. He said not a word. The moment of danger had passed. Sheriff Dunlap mopped his soaking forehead with a huge and dirty red bandanna.

"The glories of public office," he intoned.

Gardner said, "this ain't the end of this thing, men."

"I reckon not," Funeral said.

Ringbone chewed a peppermint now and he rubbed his knuckles but he said nothing. Gardner turned and left and they heard his boots move away. The sound was solid and without give.

Funeral said, "we want to go back in the cell corridor and talk with Ed Burnett, Sheriff Dunlap."

Dunlap was sitting now. He waved a hand. The motion could mean anything — despair, disgust, anger, permission. Funeral O'Neill judged it as being the last-named.

"Thanks," he murmured.

Millie Wetherford, unnoticed by the partners, had slipped into the cell area while the argument and ruckus with Gardner and Williams had been taking place, and she stood in front of the cell holding Ed Burnett when the partners came trooping down the cell aisle, boots making loud noises on the rock floor.

Ed Burnett was standing on the other side of the bars and he was wearing a wide smile when Funeral O'Neill and Ringbone Smith stopped and looked at him. He showed his infectious grin. He had a smile that always was happy, regardless of the circumstances or location.

"How are you two old buzzards?" he asked.

Funeral O'Neill said, "You look right at home, boy. Those bars really set off your homely mug."

"Ugly as a sheared sheep," Ringbone Smith joked.

Ed had both hands over Millie's hands as she grasped the bars. "Can't never boast any longer I've never been in the clink," the newspaperman said. "Look at this woman, she's sniffling."

"Oh, Ed, stop joking."

Ed Burnett grinned widely and appeared right happy. "Millie, girl, you don't want to drop tears over an old stiff like

I am – heck, woman, I'll be twenty-three, come by next birthday . . . if I'm alive." He realized one of his jokes had backfired. The fact was that he might *not* be alive to meet his next birthday. He tried another angle. "You should be happy I'm alive, even if behind bars in the Stoney Lonesome. That gunman came to my shop for one purpose . . . to kill me and kill me dead and pronto. I'm danged lucky, thanks to a lead mallet."

Funeral O'Neill spoke with philosophical dryness. "The bigger you open your mouth, my boy, the worse predicament you talk yourself into.

"Why don't you follow our pattern?" Ringbone joked. "We keep our big mouths shut."

"What a joke," Ed said.

Ringbone said, "Kiss her through the bars."

"I have long wondered," said Funeral, "if such a feat were possible."

It was. Ed kissed Millie long and fervently and Millie returned the gesture just as ardently.

"It can be done," Funeral said.

Ringbone said, "with ease, too. Now, gentlemen and young lady, let's get down to talking facts, not theories."

Millie said, "I'm having lots of trouble with my dad. He doesn't know how to straddle the fence, nor does he know which side to jump off."

"In time, he'll come around," Funeral said.

"Maybe," Millie corrected.

Ed Burnett said, "I have a newspaper to print. The type is almost all set for it, except for this murder charge – the scoop of the year here in Boxelder. The deadline is roaring down on me. The deadline is ten in the morning."

Funeral nodded. "It can wait."

"Newspapers wait for no men," the publisher corrected. "They are like tides and time. A newspaper is an odd animal. You have to live with it all the time: awake, eating, sleeping. You get one edition out and boom . . . time for the next is here. That sheet has to hit the street and the mailboxes in the postoffice tomorrow morning, men."

Funeral asked, "Where is Press Johnson?"

"Down at the shop setting type. I have to get out of here, men – I can't put out a sheet behind these bars!"

Funeral shook his head sadly. "You can't get out of here until the coroner's jury meets tomorrow morning and comes in with a verdict after all the evidence has been heard."

"You mean – that?"

"That's the law," Funeral said. "You know that as well as I do, boy."

"You're going to preside, huh, Funeral?"

"My friendship with you," the undertaker pointed out, "will have no bearing on the nature of the verdict."

Ed Burnett was very serious. "Well, reckon I have to wait, then. What time is the inquest set for?"

"We'll set it for ten in the morning."

"Deadline," the publisher said. "Reckon Press will have to get out the sheet alone. Hard work for one man."

"I'll help him," said Millie.

"Best get over there right now, then,

and get to work, honey."

Millie left.

Funeral said, "we got some questions you can answer, Ed."

"Fire away, men."

The publisher's story was brief and to the point and told the partners nothing new. Colt Hagen had come into the shop and started a fight about an editorial Ed Burnett had written and had had published.

"That extra sheet I had published yesterday," Ed Burnett explained. "It caused this trouble."

Funeral let his mind move back and remember the editorial. In it Ed Burnett had taken the cowmen to task for their blocking the coming of the farmers. He had pointed out that the prosperity of this area depended upon products from the soil and not from cattle. He had not mentioned names but a blind man could see that the editorial had been pointed toward one man and that man was Clint Gardner.

"Gardner took it as a personal insult,"

the publisher said. "So . . . he sent over his man Friday . . . Hagen called me some dirty names and although I tried not to, I got hot under the collar and told him to shut his foul mouth."

"I see," Funeral said.

"Go on," Ringbone said.

"Well, he went for his gun – don't know whether or not he meant to shoot me in cold blood – my weapon was on a table. So . . . I grappled with him. The gun went off, and grooved my thigh – not bad at all – hurts but just in the flesh. Then I got my paws on that heavy lead mallet. When it crushed his skull it made a thudding sicklike sound."

Funeral O'Neill nodded. "Did Press Johnson see the fight?"

Press Johnson was Ed's Negro pressman. "No, he was out for the minute, getting an ad from the Harness Shop. I figure that Colt arranged it so he could find me alone in the shop."

"You figure then he really meant to kill you?" Funeral O'Neill asked.

"I don't *figure* that, Funeral, I *know* he came to kill me."

The partners glanced at each other. This thing was getting rather serious. But there was nothing they could do here talking to the publisher.

"So long, Ed," Ringbone said.

Funeral said, "take it easy, boy."

"Get me out of here as fast as you can, huh?"

"We'll do our best," Funeral O'Neill assured.

They went to the sheriff's office, shutting the door behind them. Anger was in both of them. Ed Burnett was a good man – a good citizen – and he had a long and useful life ahead of him. A gunman had been hired to shorten that life, to stop the flow of strength. That gunman was dead. By luck and by strength, Ed had won that phase of his fight. But that gunman had been hired by Clint Gardner. Therefore Gardner was more to blame than was the dead Colt Hagen.

Sheriff Dunlap was alone in his office.

He sat on the bunk along the far wall and when they entered he looked up with a long and doleful and dog-sad face. Then he looked down at the corpse there on his office floor.

"What do we do with Hagen's carcass, Funeral?"

"Take him over to my funeral parlor. I'll lay him out for burial. And the bill ain't being paid for by the court taxpayers, either. Gardner will pay the bill."

"He might . . . and he might not."

Funeral said, "he'll pay."

"How will I get the carcass over to your establishment? You two aim to help me tote him?"

"Not me," Funeral said.

Ringbone said, "not me, either."

"You two sure is accommodatin'."

"We sure are," Funeral O'Neill said. They stopped at the door. "Station a deputy for a guard at Ed's cell door, Dunlap. Never for one moment leave his cell unguarded. Be sure the back door is locked all the time."

"Why all them precautions?"

"Gardner sent a gunman over to attempt to take Ed Burnett's life. His gunman failed but Gardner might try again."

"Ah, he won't make no more moves, not with Ed safe in jail."

"You heard me," Funeral said. "Station a guard there night and day."

The sheriff looked at him. Then Dunlap mopped his forehead again. "All right, Funeral, you win. I'll station a man there night and day until Burnett is either freed or convicted. But we can't hold him in jail if your jury tomorrow turns in a case of self defense."

"I know that," Funeral O'Neill said. "Where is the county attorney?"

"Out on a fishin' trip, they tell me."

"Fishing?"

"Yeah, along the crick. Took the day off. Claims fish bite good in the rain. His office man told me that."

Funeral looked at Ringbone and smiled. "Fishing . . . on the county payroll." He looked back at Dunlap. "You'd best get word to him someway about this trouble.

Has Ed Burnett seen a lawyer yet?"
"No."
"He has that right."
The sheriff said, "Now don't rush things so fast, Funeral. Things has been moving too fast anyway. There must be some easier way I can make a living than like I am, a-totin' this star."
"That's for you to figure out," Funeral said.
Ringbone said, "Come on, Funeral"
They went outside. The rain had fallen back and it was just gloomy now, with high dark clouds. A farmer named Gittler came up to them.
"How is Ed Barnett?"
"Wounded slightly in one leg," Funeral said. "Nothing serious, I understand. How are farmers taking it, Gittler?"
"The farmers won't take this very well," the man said. "They've made me Grange Leader. The Tribune is on our side. That makes Ed Burnett our friend. I've sent a messenger from farm to farm."

"For what purpose?" Ringbone Smith wanted to know.

"We meet at eight in the morning, out in the school-house on Warm Creek. Then, we ride to town – all of us – and attend the coroner's inquest. I understand the jury will consist of six men, huh?"

Funeral nodded.

"We'd sure appreciate it, sir, if three of these men were farmers."

Funeral pointed out that the prosecuting attorney and the defense attorney selected the jurors.

"I merely preside and see the trial is just and legal. But I do wish you farmers would not *all* attend."

"Why not?"

Funeral O'Neill hesitated a moment. He did not particularly like, nor did he particularly dislike, these farmers. He had lived all his life in the cow country. At the present time he and Ringbone Smith owned a good-sized cow-outfit, the range being south of Boxelder in the Bearpaw Mountains.

He and Ringbone had discussed this

question pro and con. Both were of the same opinion on one hint: here on the bottomlands and on the rolling bench-lands, the big cow-outfits were through. This land could not be farmed. The empire was moving West, always West. More farmers would come. More fences, more plowed land, more houses. And the farmers were settled legally, having made homestead entries under the government's Homestead Act.

The cowmen did not own deeds to land over which their herds grazed. Had they owned this land they would have had to pay taxes and the range was so poor and the cattle so low in beef-poundage these taxes would be hard to pay. To stay in business the cowman would have to graze his stock over land which cost him nothing or very little.

If he had to pay taxes, this would take the profit out of the cow business. Funeral and his partner had it figured out. The cowmen would have to move back into the rough country — the brakes and mountains, where a plow was of no use. Then, too, the quality of the cattle had to he improved. These cattle were offsprings of Texas longhorns, driven up the Powder River Trail, and they had bones and horns, but very little beef for the size of their frames. They would have to be bred up to the point where each steer turned over twice or three times the beef on the same amount of grass and hay.

"There might be trouble," Funeral said.

Gittler was silent for a moment. Funeral pegged him as a man having more than good sense. Evidently the farmers thought so, also, for had they not chosen him as their leader? But one element somewhat puzzled the undertaker. Gittler had not used his brains when selecting his homestead site. He had a wife and three children, and he had failed on a worthless piece of land back in the rougher country – a black igneous rimrock cap stretched across his farm, and this could not be farmed. Funeral blamed this error in selection upon the man's ignorance of farming and land values, for plainly Gittler had been a city man. He and Ringbone had wondered at this selection for a homestead but both had said nothing to Gittler. It was none of their business.

"What do you mean?" Gittler asked.

"You know what I mean," the undertaker said. "Clint Gardner wants trouble with you farmers. This range is strung as tight as a fiddle-string. One move – one bad word – and the hell will break loose."

Gittler nodded, eyes sober. "But we have to stand up for our rights," he was quick to point out.

"I'm not consenting that point," Funeral reminded. "I am merely stating my viewpoint. All of you farmers get in a group and Gardner will get his cowpunchers in a group and a few drinks of whiskey will go around and boom – there'll be some widows and orphans."

Gittler nodded.

Ringbone Smith said, "This is none of

our business, fellow. We're only offering advice. Gardner has some tough men – born and raised in the cow-country – and they hate two types of people, sheepherders and farmers. There might be a mess of gun-play, Mr. Gittler."

"I'll – think it over."

"We got to abide by the law," Funeral said.

Gittler spoke with hoarse rapidness. "Gardner don't abide by the law. He sent Colt Hagen down to kill Ed Burnett."

"We can't prove that," Funeral said.

"You two don't talk like you are such good friends to Ed Burnett as Ed claims you are. Maybe he was mistaken all the time, huh?"

Funeral held back his anger. A glance at Ringbone showed that his partner's full face had become blank and that he did not chew his peppermint. Funeral returned his gaze to the farmer.

"That is our business, Gittler. Your business is with your farmers. But use your discretion and lead them to peace . . . and not bloodshed."

"You got a big responsibility," Ringbone Smith said.

The partners left the farmer standing there, and Ringbone Smith was muttering something about *arrogance.* Funeral merely let his partner mumble. He looked across Boxelder's main street. Lawyer Andy Mills stood in front of his office talking to Matthew Davis, a farmer from up on Clear Creek. The young lawyer saw Funeral's glance, and lifted his hand.

"Him and Ed Burnett are good friends," Ringbone Smith said, seeing the exchange of gestures, "and I suppose he will defend Ed, huh?"

"Reckon so."

At this juncture, two men came out of Sheriff Dunlap's office, carrying the limp body of Colt Hagen between them, the body sagging like a broken sack of wheat. Men removed their hats in respect to the corpse. But actually, they were not honoring Hagen; they were doffing hats in respect to Death. When they went past the undertaker, the lead man grunted, "Is your parlor door open, Funeral?"

"lt is unlocked. Take him inside and put him on the table." The man continued on, panting under his load. "Ready for the needle, huh," he said, and cackled.

Clint Gardner came out of the Mercantile. He walked the way a man of importance walks – noticing nobody. But Funeral O'Neill made it a point to see that the cowman *noticed* him, for he stepped in front of Gardner, who had to stop.

"I'd like a word with you, Gardner."

"About this printer – and this murder?"

"No, about something else."

Displeasure ran across the predatory face, had its moment, and then became submerged under the guise of conviviality.

"What else, O'Neill?"

Clint Gardner had the abrupt manner of a busy man doling out a few words to an inferior person or a hireling of his. This registered on the bony undertaker and added no sugar to his already salty personality. But Funeral O'Neill was not one to tip his hand too easily and when he spoke only Ringbone, his close friend, could tell and detect the animosity in Funeral's tone of voice.

"A few weeks back, Mr. Gardner, one of your hands got killed when a bucking horse went over backwards with him, crushing him under the saddle horn. I laid that boy away and buried him. You promised to pay the bill. I sent you that bill. So far you haven't paid me."

"This is only the sixth of the month."

Funeral shook his head dolefully. "The sum was due for payment the first. You are six days late in meeting this obligation."

People had stopped and were shamelessly listening. One of the farmers, apparently not over burdened with brains, laughed a little. And, for some reason, the laugh sounded sinister, and ugly. Gardner glanced at the man and anger touched his face, pulling at the corners of his thin-lipped mouth.

"You'll get your check, undertaker."

"Yes," said Funeral, "I'll get it eventually. I've had trouble collecting from you before. But I'll make sure I'm paid before I bury Colt Hagen."

Gardner watched him, eyes moving tighter. "Are you siding with these hoemen, too, O'Neill? Are you forgettin' that King Cow, not a Walking plow, made this town, built up this country?"

"I'm forgetting nothing." Funeral was brusque. "I have my own thoughts. They are my business, and the business of nobody else."

Their gazes met. Gardner smiled then, and the smile was forced. "I'll write you a check in the bank. I'm going there on some business. I'll have somebody deliver it to you. No, I'll mail it to you."

"Thanks," Funeral said.

He had spoken very slowly, very deliberately, and in a very dry voice. Gardner said no more. He wheeled about, a man heavy with importance, and he walked toward the bank, boots vicious on the worn plank sidewalk.

Lawyer Andy Smith had crossed the street to watch and listen. Now he smiled boyishly and said, "You doused a bucket of cold water over the local cattle king, Funeral."

"Have you been down to the jail to see Ed yet?"

"No."

"I figure he'll hire you for a lawyer."

"He has no other choice," Smith pointed out, smiling widely. "The only other attorney in town is the county attorney and he can't defend the man while he is prosecuting him."

"Why haven't you been down to see Ed?"

Smith's smile widened. "Rain always makes me sleepy. Rain drops off eaves, and it sounds so peaceful . . . To tell the truth, the whole truth, and nothing but the truth, I just woke up, Funeral. I have a cot in my office. I became overpowered by lassitude. Therefore I missed the whole shebang."

"You sure are a wide-awake lawyer."

Andy Smith kept on smiling. "I got the nap-habit from a local person," he said. "A mortician." Suddenly he stopped speaking, mouth half open. He was staring at a point down the street beyond Funeral O'Neill. Others, catching his surprise, wheeled, looking down the street, and Funeral turned also.

They were gawking at the building housing the Boxelder Tribune. It was a frame building badly in need of paint, and storm and rain and sun had buffeted it, giving it a shaky appearance. But what had attracted the young attorney's attention was not the physical appearance of Ed Burnett's printing establishment.

What had attracted their attention was this: From under the eaves of the roof, smoke was belching forth.

"Fire!" a man screamed.

Like most pioneer towns, Boxelder had a volunteer fire-department. This consisted of a five hundred gallon drum of water on a wagon. The wagon and its load of water were always outside the livery-barn. The citizens had asked Funeral O'Neill to be fire-chief some years before but he had eased the responsibilities over on his partner who now hollered for the volunteers to get to the livery-barn and hook a team onto the water-wagon.

The entire town came to quick life. For months it had been walking the tightrope of danger and uncertainty. Now the demand for instant action broke this tension, and men and women were ready to go to work against a common foe.

"Somebody get a team out to the livery-barn," Ringbone Smith ordered. "Hook onto the water wagon and get it down the street. Then get some buckets – everybody get a bucket – and we'll have a bucket-brigade."

Two men were already harnessing a team. Harnesses lifted and went down, belly-bands were snapped, and tugs were linked onto the double-tree of the wagon, and other hands put up the neckyoke. Then a man was on the seat and hollering, "Make tracks, horses, make tracks!"

The wagon careened around a corner, skidded wildly in the dust, and then the team, ears back, was hammering toward the burning building.

By the time the water-wagon had

arrived, Funeral O'Neill and Ringbone Smith were at the burning building. Funeral had almost fallen when he had run over Mrs. Chesterfield's mutt. He had almost broke one of his legs and his boot had done no good to the cur's ribs. The dog had gone away at a wild run, yipping as he sought his home.

They had tried to get in the front door, but the door was locked. That was an odd thing indeed, for the newspaper had been open for business — or, at least, it should have been open. They had rammed their bodies against the door but it had held firm. It was a heavy door made of logs bolted together and it was evidently latched securely inside, a bar across it.

The door had been barred from the inside.

The thought came that Old Press had locked the door to keep out any visitors while the old Negro worked on putting out the next issue of the Tribune. Funeral wondered if the old man were in the burning building. He thought a lot of Old Press. Old Press had worked for Ed Burnett's predecessor and Funeral and Ringbone had known the printer for many years.

"Press Johnson is in there," Ringbone hollered. He had gone to a window and had cupped his hands and peered into the printing shop. "I kin see him a layin' there on the floor. Reckon the smoke must've overcome him, huh?"

"We got to get him out," Funeral said.

"How?"

"Back door."

Funeral headed for the alley with Ringbone Smith behind him. Many a friendly cribbage game had been staged by the old printer and the undertaker. Funeral hurried, Ringbone trotting behind him. By luck there was a vacant lot on each side of the Tribune office. Therefore the fire would not be too hard to contain unless the wind increased in velocity. Funeral wondered, "Wonder what started the fire?" and Ringbone Smith, apparently bothered by the same question, said. "They ain't never had no cause to use any fire in this outfit except to melt down lead, and that is done in a kind of a forge Ed made."

"The back door is open," Funeral said.

"Why didn't Old Press make a run for it, I wonder?"

"Smoke might have overcome him too soon."

"You don't reckon he's dead?"

"Hope not, Ringbone."

Smoke rolled out the wide door. It hit the outside air, thinned out, and the wind blew it away.

"I got to go in there," Funeral said.

Suddenly a man called, "Don't go in there, O'Neill. You'll never come out alive, man – that joint is really burning."

Funeral noticed that the speaker was Williams, the man who had tried to keep him from entering Sheriff Dunlap's office – the man he and Ringbone Smith had both knocked down.

"Don't worry about us," Funeral said.

"I tried to get in there," Williams

hollered. "I was the one what opened that door. But the smoke – it's too thick – "

Funeral was driven out of the doorway by the black rolling smoke. By this time other people were in the alley. Sheriff Dunlap was organizing a bucket-brigade. The town windmill was wide open. Men and women and children were getting in two lines of humanity between the fire and the windmill. One line would move the empty buckets toward the windmill; the other line would move the buckets back filled with water. But some of the people were crowding too close.

"Get back there," the sheriff hollered. "Get in that bucket-line, all of you. Man alive, Funeral, but that smoke looks black. Black as pitch. Looks like oil is burnin' in there, to make smoke that black."

"Old Press Johnson is in there," a man hollered. A woman sobbed, "Oh, somebody – please – Get him out of there. He might still be alive!"

A man hurried up with an armful

of gunny sacks. The smoke seemed to momentarily subside. Funeral knew he had to do something and do it soon. He grabbed one of the sacks and doused it in a bucket of water. It soaked the water like a sponge.

"Throw a couple of buckets of water over me," the undertaker ordered. "Douse me to the hide and do it quick."

"You ain't on fire, O'Neill."

"Throw water on me, quick – and ask no fool questions."

"You goin' in there, Funeral?" Dunlap asked.

"Going to try."

Three bucketsful of water, manned by three men, cascaded down on the undertaker, and one hit him in the face, driving the breath from him. Within a moment or two he was saturated to the skin and dripping water. Ringbone brought the gunny sack out of the water; it dropped and was soggy.

"I'll go with you, Funeral."

"Stay out, Ringbone. One man is enough – "

Sheriff Dunlap grabbed the mortician's arm. His fingers were bands of steel. "Funeral, don't rush in there, please."

"Mostly smoke and hardly any fire," Funeral said. "I got to get him out of there. He's my old cribbage opponent. And a man can't afford to let a good cribbage player die. They're too hard to find, too valuable."

"They sure don't seem to be much fire," a man hollered. "Mostly pitch black smoke, looks to me."

"Here we go," Funeral said.

He held the wet gunny sack across his nose and mouth. He peered over the top of the sack. Then he plunged into the smoke. The acrid smoke cut through the wet sacking and hit his lungs. He wanted to cough but he kept himself from coughing. He went down low, and this way the smoke rolled over him; closer to the floor, the smoke was not so dense. He went forward, bent at the waist. He did not feel much heat. There was lots of coiling smoke.. .but little heat. Then he saw fire ahead of him. One wall was beginning to burn. The fire was eating into the wall, starting down on the mopboards. He found himself coughing. He pulled the wet gunny sack up over his nose again. Then through the smoke he caught sight of Press Johnson. The man lay on his belly there on the floor.

"I'm behind you, Funeral."

The voice belonged to Ringbone Smith. Funeral could not see his partner. But he hollered above the crackle of the flames.

"Get out of here. Get some water. We can put this out if we get in here and get to work. Don't let them blast open the front door. The fire will get air then; we got to keep it stifled."

"I'll go out, Funeral."

The smoke coiled and circulated, rising and rolling toward the open back door. He was glad the fire was not huge and had not spread much. Had there been much fire, he could never have entered the building; heat would have driven him back. He was on his hands and knees now beside the printer. He could hear people talking and hollering out in the alley. The sounds were dim and remote; they seemed to come from another world — a world far away without smoke. A world unobscured by ropes of black and swirling smoke.

He started to cough again and he bent over, head close to the floor, for there was oxygen down along the floor. For a moment he wondered if he had not bit off more than he could chew. But he got the smoke out of his lungs and he hollered, "Throw in a rope, quick. Just heave it through the door. I haven't got strength to pull him out. Hurry, damn it, hurry!"

"Funeral wants a rope!"

"Rope coming up."

He crawled forward on his hands and knees. His fingers found Press Johnson's ankles. He tried to pull the man forward. But the smoke had got the best of him and the man was heavy. Lying as he was on the floor, he almost had a lot of friction between his body and the rough flooring. Then Funeral O'Neill was hit from behind. And then the rope lay beside him.

"You get the rope, Funeral?" a voice demanded, smashing through the black smoke.

"Got it, friend."

"Tie it around his legs and we'll pull him out. We got hold of the other end. You hang onto the rope, too, and we'll take you out with it."

"Not me, men."

"Why not?"

"This fire can be put out easy if water is brought in. Ringbone, where the heck are you, partner?"

"Coming, Funeral."

Funeral had the rope tied around the pressman's ankles.

"Pull," he ordered.

The rope tightened and Old Press skidded toward the door. Funeral did not have time to put him on his back. The thought came that by the time Old Press reached the door, he'd have lots of slivers in his face, seeing his face was bumping over the rough floor. But maybe the man was already dead and would not feel the slivers? Funeral did not like this idea one bit.

Where was Ringbone Smith?

Funeral found himself angry with the slowness of his partner. A few pails of water would douse this fire before it really got a start; so far it was mostly smoke. Fire must have broken out in the waste basket, he figured. There Old Press and Ed Burnett had thrown pieces of wastecloth used in cleaning their hands and the press. These must have suffered spontaneous combustion. They were soaked with oil and grease; this smoke was an oily and greasy smoke.

He seemed all alone in the world. Although he could hear the babble of voices from the alley, they seemed not a part of him or his world. He lay on his belly and inched toward the box of waste cloths. It was burning merrily. Smoke belched from it. The box was made of steel. The flames were eating into the wall. But a few buckets of water – applied to the wall immediately – They would kill the flames. The water would bounce down into the box and kill the fire there.

Was there anything he could do?

He saw a box of sand over by a bench. He wondered, idly, what sand was doing in a print shop, and then he remembered that sometimes the town women would leave their children with Ed Burnett, while they visited or shopped. The kids had the sand to play with. He crept toward the box. He got a handful of sand and threw it on the box of blazing rags. This did some good – for a moment the fire hesitated, then grew again. He pulled the sand over to the center of the floor. Smoke and coughing nauseated him and prostrated him. The thought came that he might have been foolish for not going out with the rope when it had been pulled out with Old Press on the end of it. But that was too late, now.

"Ringbone, barge in here, man."

"Coming, with two buckets."

He heard the sound of boots. He got

BR5

to his feet and out of the smoke came the lunging form of his partner, a bucket of water in each hand. Ringbone almost fell, but he got low on the floor, coughing. Funeral waited no longer. One bucket of water was slapped down on the burning rags. They stopped burning instantly. Then, to make sure, the other bucket went on the rags, too. This killed most of the smoke. But they needed more water. You could see the flames clearly now. They were eating merrily into the dried wall.

"Water," hollered the mortician.

Ringbone Smith was sitting up, his coughing spell gone. "Them rags caused most of it," he said, spitting as he talked. "Must have caught a-fire of their own accord. Barge in with water, men. The smoke is going."

From the back door came a roaring voice. "All right, men and neighbors, you heard them – get that water in there. Here, I'll lead the way".

Funeral said, "That was Clint Gardner's sweet little voice."

"This don't make logic," Ringbone said.

"I reckon not," Funeral said, "but human nature is an odd animal. Gardner is Ed Burnett's enemy and now he wants to save Ed's property."

"Right neighborly of him, I'd say."

"Something," said Funeral, "smells of fish."

"I think so too."

"Wonder if Old Press is alive or dead?"

"I don't know."

Now the smoke was leaving and human forms were breaking through it. The worst of the dirty work was done. From now on, water would take over. Buckets went down the empty line to the tank, were filled, and then went from hand to hand down the full line. Then the buckets went into the Tribune Office and hit the fire. The smoke died and the water had won its fight. The first man into the building had been nobody but Clint Gardner. Behind Gardner had come Williams. Funeral O'Neill had aching eyes and throbbing lungs and he was so full of smoke he could hardly breathe, but despite these impediments he thought the actions of the two Circle S men were rather out of pattern. They were fighting hard to save the property of a man they hated – a man they had sent one of their gunmen out to kill . . .

Then another explanation came to the mortician's throbbing brain. Gardner owned a few buildings here in Boxelder and perhaps he fought this hard for the purpose of keeping the fire from spreading and getting to his property. Had this fire been allowed to progress, had the wind become stronger – well, Gardner might have lost some property.

Funeral rubbed his eyes and let it go at that. He had many years ago learned that the human being is a thing of frailty, both in body and in purpose and in mind; things happened, and there was no way to rush time or fate. He was doing nothing in here so he turned and went out. He did not know it but he lurched and once in the alley, a man caught him and held him. A woman thrust a bucketful of cold water under his nose and said, "Drink, Funeral, drink."

"With pleasure, Mrs. Flannigan."

The water tumbled down his throat. It was ice cold and smoke and lassitude vanished under its magic influence. He looked at Ringbone Smith who sat across the alley with his back to a shed and who had just lowered a bucket of water. His partner was dirty with soot and smoke and his face was streaked with sweat and soot.

"Hope I don't look as bad as you," the undertaker joked.

"You look like a pile of charred wood."

"We're kinda too stove-up to play this hero stuff," the mortician said, "but we did it. Hey, doc, is Old Press with us, or is he out of this world?"

The doctor was kneeling beside the printer who lay on his back with his mouth wide open. His eyes were open, too, but they saw nothing – they were huge white marbles protruding from the ink-black face.

Funeral wobbled over and looked down at his old friend. He had seen hundreds of dead men, and he had the ability to determine almost at a glance whether life had deserted the human carcass.

"He's just out, huh, doc?"

"You got eyes, ain't you?" The doctor passed a vial of ammonia under the printer's nose. Funeral got a whiff of it despite the distance. "He's out cold as a cucumber is supposed to be."

"Anything else wrong with him?"

"Got a bump on the back of his cranium."

"Oh."

"Oh what?"

Funeral grinned. "You're in a right pleasant mood, doc." He got to his knees and ran a hand under the Negro's head. His fingers felt gingerly along the base of the skull. His hand came out with some blood on it and some mud on it, too. Then the mortician stood up and had a long dour face. By now the smoke had left him and he was almost his old physical self.

"Something has smacked him along the base of his skull," the mortician said. "Knocked him out. He's got some blood but his skull is as solid and hard as a saddle's tree, so no fracture."

"Are you the doctor, or am I?"

"Go to hell," Funeral said.

"Come with me," the doc said.

"This country," said Ringbone, "is really getting tough. The undertaker and the doctor lighting. You two have worked together for years, too. Too bad . . . And some even go so far as to claim you rebated the doctor because the men and women he kills for you, Funeral."

"You are not funny," Funeral said.

The doctor did not even answer. He evidently had had enough trouble for one day. First, the dead man — Colt Hagen; then a wounded man, Ed Burnett; now a fire and a man overcome by smoke.

Funeral was aware that Clint Gardner stood beside him with Williams a pace behind his boss.

"Fire all out," Gardner said. "Them rags must have caught on fire by themselves."

"Soaked in grease and oil," Williams said.

Gardner looked down at Press Johnson. "Heard you say he had some blood on the back of his head."

"He has."

"Smoke might have caught him unaware and he might have fallen on something when he hit the floor."

"There's a spilled case of type in there," Williams said.

Gardner said, "Might have clipped his head on it when he went down." He was grimy and he smelled of smoke. His face had streaks of black. "Well, we saved the town, men. That fire, had it got away, might have razed the town."

Funeral merely nodded.

Funeral went into the printing establishment, with Ringbone Smith walking beside him. There was the smell of water and smoke and soot. The floor was dirty with water and ashes. People were milling around. Funeral and Ringbone hazed the people outside and were alone in the fire-hit building.

Funeral glanced at the floor whereon Old Press had been lying. He saw nothing there that the man could have hit his head against unless, on falling, the back of his head had hit the floor, and he doubted this – the blow seemed to have apparently come from something smashing, something that had hit hard and had broken the skin.

"Wonder what he socked his skull on?" Ringbone asked.

"I don't know." Funeral moved over and looked at the bunch of burned-out waste in the metal box. His mind was active. Clint Gardner had sent Colt Hagen to kill Ed Burnett. Hagen had failed. Gardner had to get rid of the Tribune. Fire was one way to rid himself of his enemy. Burn down his building, melt his type, ruin his old printing machine. But Gardner had worked to overcome the flames. Well, that made him look good, anyway. Took suspicion from his shoulders. Funeral grinned in wry ugliness.

Seriously he doubted the theory that the waste rags had broken out in spontaneous combustion. Ed Burnett was cleaniness and carefulness personified,as was Old Press. But still, an accident was an accident . . . But it would have been easy for a man to sneak in the back door and lay a blackjack across the base of Old Press' skull, for the printer was somewhat hard of hearing. Then a match, tossed into the waste-rags.

Ringbone said. "That fire has spread along them mopboards, Funeral. And that, to me, is not logical. Fire burns up, not down."

"Not so loud," Funeral said.

Ringbone lowered his voice. "Could have been some kerosene sprinkled along them mopcards. Then when the fire started in the waste it could have jumped out, hit the kerosene, and licked along the walls."

"Don't talk about it here, because there are too many ears around."

Williams left his group, across the room, for a few men had come back in, and he came forward, and he said, "There's a block of lead over there on the floor, men. Old Press might have hit his head against it when he fell."

Funeral saw a block of lead about eight inches long and about four inches wide and about the same in height. It had not been on the floor a moment before. Evidently Williams had hooked it out from under the bench with the toe of his boot and had shoved it forward. Funeral was not sure. But he was pretty sure it had not been on the floor, when he had looked.

"That could have happened," a man said.

Funeral said nothing. He lifted his eyes for a moment and met the eyes of his partner, and Ringbone Smith said, "He might have done that, men."

Funeral had a rough thought — Williams was lying. He had deliberately toed that block out from under the bench. He had fooled the townspeople but not Funeral or Ringbone. Another thought gripped him: Maybe this was a blind to get the people to the fire and then somebody would sneak into the jail and murder Ed Burnett. And because of the commotion and noise around the fire the sound of the shooting would pass unnoticed?

Funeral hurried outside, Ringbone followed him. They were in the alley. "Go to the jail and check on Ed," the mortician ordered.

"Oh, Lord," the veterinarian said, and hurried away. He was almost running. The fact had dawned on him, too. Old Press was coming out of it. Within a few minutes, Ringbone Smith was back, breathing hard from his run.

"Millie had the same idea," he said.

"She at the jail?"

"With a rifle," Ringbone Smith said. He pulled a peppermint from his vest pocket. He looked at it. It had originally been white. Smoke had turned it dark brown. "But it's still good." The peppermint hit his mouth.

"Millie was in the corridor, huh?"

"Yeah." Ringbone kept his voice low. "She claims she saw the back doorknob turn. But she had locked the door. It had been unlocked when she had come in. The jail office — Dunlap's office — it had been empty."

"Somebody could have walked in and murdered Ed."

"If she hadn't been there, yes."

"Did she see who it was that tried the door?"

"Nope. No glass in the door. No way to look out into the alley. Winders weren't in the right spot." Ringbone looked at Old Press, who was sitting up with a dazed look on his face, bottom lip hanging down and trembling. "I wonder if he won't have something to tell us?"

"I doubt that."

"Why say that?"

"He's hard of hearing. Somebody could come up behind him and slug him cold easily. I doubt if he saw who it was . . . if he was slugged."

"On what do you base that?"

"If he'd seen who had slugged him, that man would have killed him to silence him. Well, that's the way it looks to me."

"We might be using too much imagination."

"I doubt it."

"Press might know something," Ringbone said stubbornly.

Old Press was a weary man with a huge headache. The print-shop smelled of ink, water, paper, and ashes. The doors were closed and Funeral and his partner and Old Press were the only people in the workshop. From the alley came the talk of children and grown-ups who were talking this over. Funeral O'Neill could hear the murmur of their voices. But his interest was not stationed on the sounds. His interest was centered on Old Press, who sat in the chair.

"What happened to you, Press?"

The printer looked up with round eyes. A dark set of fingers, darker yet because of the ink on them, gingerly felt the back of his skull, then came down and cradled the dark head.

"My head, Funeral, is bustin'."

"Them headache powders will take effect soon," Ringbone Smith said around a peppermint. "Can you tell us what happened, man?"

"No I can't."

"Why not?" Funeral wanted to know.

"Because I don't know what happened."

"Tell us what you do know?" encouraged. the undertaker.

The Negro talked in rumbling tones. "I was standin' there at the table settin' some type. All of a sudden everything goes black – I thinks the sun is settin' right early. Next thing I know I'm out in the alley smellin' that junk the doctor held under my nostrils." He shook his head slowly. "My head is gettin' to feel better, at that."

"You don't remember anything else?"

"Not a thing, Funeral."

"You never saw the guy who slugged you?"

"I might not have been slugged. I might just have fainted. I dunno."

"You been having dizzy spells lately?" Ringbone asked.

"Me? Dizzy spells? I'm as healthy as a work-horse, Mr. Ringbone."

"Do you figure you might have got slugged?" Funeral asked.

"I don't know one way or the other."

Funeral O'Neill glanced at his partner. Ringbone owned a long and horsey-looking face. They were up against the proverbial blank wall. Somebody pounded on the back door.

"Let us in," a voice said.

"Sheriff Dunlap," Ringbone Smith said.

Funeral said, "let the pest in."

With the sheriff were two men – Clint Gardner and Williams. Dunlap wanted to further question Old Press Johnson. Gardner and Williams apparently had no questions to ask. Dunlap got nothing out of the printer. Gardner watched, face without thoughts, and occasionally he touched his cigaret, lightly pulling in the smoke. Williams stood in dogged and glum silence.

"You're kinda excited," Dunlap said at length. "You don't remember just what did happen, looks like to me: You might've got excited when the fire broke loose in that rag box, and started for it and stumbled on that lead and fell down and knocked yourself cold."

"They wasn't no fire when I passed out," the printer corrected.

"You was meltin' down some lead," the sheriff said. "You admit that yourself. That might have caught fire — that lead pot is close to them rags — fumes might have caught fire from the fire under the lead pot."

"I don't remembers."

Gardner said. "Why question the poor fellow. He's had a rough day, as it is. Let the man be. He might have fainted. He might have stumbled and knocked himself out. I say let him get his bearings."

"Good idea," Funeral said.

Williams looked at Clint Gardner. "Reckon it's time we headed out for the ranch, huh, Clint?"

Gardner shook his head. "I'm staying

in town tonight, Williams. You head out to the ranch." The rancher looked at Sheriff Dunlap, let his eyes move to Ringbone Smith, then back to Funeral O'Neill. "He might have fainted. He's not a young man any longer. He could have toppled into the heater and got it on the floor."

"It was on the floor when I first came in," Gardner said.

Funeral O'Neill had noticed that, also. "A good bit of thinking," he said. He looked at the old printer. "Could that have happened Old Press?"

"Anything could have happened, Funeral."

Williams said, "Well, me for the long ride," and he went out.

Old Press Johnson said, "No rest for the wicked, I reckon. Although my head has got half a dozen Sioux bucks in there dancing the war-dance with tom-toms going, I still have a paper to publish and a deadline."

"Got to get along now," Gardner said. "Hope you come out of this okay, Old

Press. You have my sympathies."

"Thank you, sir."

Gardner also left. Funeral O'Neill glanced at the man's straight back and thought, he's a smart one, and let it go at that. Sheriff Dunlap was peering at the burned area on the wall. He was offering estimates of how much it would cost to repair the building. Ringbone Smith chewed his peppermints and said nothing. His gaze met that of Funeral. Ringbone Smith saw a long face and he had expected his partner's eyes to show something – but they were lifeless and dull and without anything.

Funeral spoke to Sheriff Dunlap. "Where is that deputy you said was going to stand guard over Ed Burnett's cell, Dunlap?"

Dunlap wheeled, something in the undertaker's voice turning him sharply. "He's over to the jail on his job. Why ask?"

"He wasn't there when the fire took place."

"How do you know?"

"I saw him . . . . out in the crowd."

Dunlap's face became severe. "By golly, he was out there – he was . . . I remember seeing him now. I'll talk to him." The lines left. "But there ain't no use havin' a guard all night and day over a man in as safe a place as a jail."

"Hagen tried to kill him, remember?" Funeral was quick to point out.

Ringbone Smith rolled his peppermint between green-stained teeth. He knew his partner wanted to get rid of Dunlap so he could continue his talk with Old Press, who stood at a type-case and occasionally sent slanting glances toward Funeral O'Neill. Dunlap was chewing again, jaws thin vises clamping down on the tobacco.

"I'll go over and check on that deputy and on Ed," the sheriff said.

Funeral said, "Good idea."

The sheriff left but the trio was not left alone, for another man entered. He was the farmer Gittler. He went right to the point.

"What you got to say, Press?"
"What do you mean, president of the Grangers?"
"What happened?"
Some roughness in the man's voice irritated Funeral O'Neill. This man had one of Gardner's bad traits, too much arrogance. So the undertaker went to bat for the printer.
"Press has a whale of a headache, Gittler. He doesn't feel like talking. Besides, he has a newspaper to set and publish."
Gittler frowned. He looked at the printer. Then his eyes swung around and settled on Funeral O'Neill.
"Let's get something straight, O'Neill." Did his voice hold a subtle threat? "I'm a farmer. Because I am a farmer I am automatically Clint Gardner's enemy. This newspaper is fighting Gardner. Therefore it and its publisher and workers are my friends."
"Simple mathematics," Funeral murmured. "Continue, Gittler?"
"Colt Hagen came over to kill Burnett.

By luck it is Colt on your slab . . . and not Ed."

"We all know that," Funeral gently reminded. "Get to your point, Gittler?"

Gittler rubbed his whiskery jaw. It sounded like a boar rubbing against a post. "Don't push me, undertaker . . . I figure this establishment didn't catch fire by accident. I figure this printer was slugged from behind – he's hard of hearing – and I figure this fire was set by Gardner or one of his men."

Funeral O'Neill studied the farmer. For some reason he got the impression that this man, though his blunt statements, expected blunt, yet revealing, answers. That meant, then, Gittler was fishing for information. Funeral toyed with this thought. He decided then and there, he would like to know more about Fred Gittler. About the man's past life, his place of residence. Clint Gardner was no fool. Gardner was a smart man. He was smart enough to place a spy in the midst of the farmers – a turncoat who apparently bucked him but who, all the time, was on his side and was drawing his wages.

This was just a hunch.

Nothing more.

But Funeral O'Neill knew full well the value of a hunch. He had followed them before and many times they had paid off. Would this hunch materialize?

"You can't prove a word you say, Gittler," he pointed out.

"I know that. But, just the same, I'm saying what I think. It could be possible, you know."

"Yes, it could be," Funeral assured.

"Might be so," Ringbone Smith murmured.

Fred Gittler was silent for a moment, apparently, undecided, then he turned and said, "So long, men."

He left by the front door, which had been unbarred.

"Just the three of us," Ringbone Smith said softly.

Funeral O'Neill gestured toward the back door but said nothing. Ringbone walked to the door, making no noise, and looked out. He came back and said, "Nobody eavesdropping Shylock."

"Sherlock," Funeral corrected.

Ringbone shook his head. "Shylock," he insisted. Old Press rubbed his nose. He looked at Ringbone and then moved his eyes over to Funeral O'Neill.

"I don't know a thing more, men, I told you all of it. I was settin' type and then the sun goes down but the moon don't come up."

"Was the back door open?" Funeral asked.

"She was wide open, men. That lead I was meltin' down had a lot of ink in it and it stunk tremendous." Grimy fingers searched the case for the letter S. "Front door was wide open, too."

"The front door," Funeral corrected, "was barred from the inside."

Press Johnson forgot the letter S. He looked down at them and his bottom lip trembled. "You – sure about that?"

"We tried to break in that door," the undertaker said.

The man's bottom lip vibrated like a

leaf in a storm. His eyes became wide and showed fear.

"Then, by golly, somebody has sneaked in and slugged me and set this fire, and they has barred the door so nobody could come in accidently on them. They're tried to kill me . . . jes' like they done tried to kill my boss."

"Take it easy," the mortician soothed.

The lip stopped trembling. It became rigid. "I'm going to get me a pelt to tan for my parlor wall . . . the pelt of a gent named Clint Gardner."

Funeral O'Neill spoke almost sternly. "Put such things out of your cranium, Old Press. Ed Burnett is our friend, too."

The Negro looked at him. There was a silence. Then Old Press said, "Wonder why ol' man Quinn ain't arrove yet?"

"What about him?" asked Ringbone.

"He done went out for a bottle of beer for me. Went to the saloon. I gave him the money right afore my lights went out."

"The old souse has probably drunk the beer himself," Funeral O'Neill said.

"You can kiss that money good-by."

The printer shook his head stubbornly. "I don't agree with you, Funeral. Ol' Quinn has done run beer errands for me for years. He still has the first time not to come back with his goal." He frowned and rubbed his head. "I heard you mention that they was a hunk of lead layin' on the floor. Is thet right?"

"There was," Ringbone Smith said.

"I never leaves no lead on the floor. Never have left no lead there, men."

"Just another old drunk," Ringbone snorted.

But Funeral O'Neill was busy in thought. The idea of the beer seemed to fascinate him, and he put his thoughts into words.

"So Quinn sent out for a bottle, huh? And then you got knocked cold – or whatever happened to you . . . And you haven't seen Quinn since?"

"Ain't seen him." Press Johnson crossed the room. His long arms almost to his knees. "Don't know what could have happend to him. Usually he is almighty prompt."

There came a knock at the front door. Old Press admitted a short man with a huge belly. He sank into a chair and sighed. Then he said, "Hello, men."

Funeral made no attempt to keep the sarcasm out of his voice. "How is the fishing, County Attorney Parnell?"

Lazy deep eyes lifted and touched him. They seemed to own a solid impact. The thick lips moved slowly.

"I don't quite follow you, Funeral. What are you driving at?"

Funeral grinned. "Sheriff Dunlap spilled the beans on you, Parnell. Said you had gone fishing. You've missed a lot of excitement."

Attorney George Parnell nodded absently. "Dunlap is an unmitigated idiot. He would make a good volcano inspector." He fumbled in his vest pocket and came out with a short cigar. "I hate to prosecute young Ed Burnett. He's my friend – a good friend. But . . . it's my job as a county attorney. Hell when a man has to move against his friends."

"The coroner's inquest," reminded Funeral O'Neill, "has not been held yet. If Ed is absolved of all blame, then there is no need for prosecution."

Parnell nodded, seemingly interested in his stogie. He was a lazy man and he liked to boast of his laziness but he had graduated high at the top of his class in a big eastern university. He stayed in Boxelder because he liked to fish and hunt and he had a small ranch on the north edge of the valley. Funeral liked him. He was a good county attorney. He interfered in nobody's business unless that business became detrimental to the public he was hired to protect.

"That is correct," Parnell said.

Funeral got to his feet. "I have to get to the post office," he said, "because I'm expecting a check from Gardner."

The lawyer spoke without life. "The three sweetest words known to man's ears. *Enclosed find check.*" He swung his eyes on Ringbone Smith. "You'll answer my questions, huh? I've got to get both sides of this problem, you know."

"I have to go with Funeral."

The lawyer shook his head in feigned disgust. He spoke to the world in general and nobody in particular.

"And they have the nerve to call themselves citizens . . . Yet they work not an iota to bring about justice." He seemed made of blubber and he was apparently relaxed, a fat man without starch or backbone, but this was only a pretense. "Ringbone Smith, sit down and talk to me."

"Shoot, Parnell," he said.

Funeral left them then and went to the post office. True to his promise, Clint Gardner had mailed him a check, and he took it from his box with a grin. The check was scrawled in hard rough handwriting that bespoke of anger and impatience. Funeral studied it, saw the sum was correct, folded it and put it in his shirt pocket. Then he addressed his words to the postmaster.

"Have you seen old man Quinn around?"

The man had not seen Quinn recently. Funeral nodded, gave the information proper scope and attention, and the postmaster, who was a gossipy old son, wanted to know why he wanted to see Quinn.

"Got a bottle of whiskey I want to give him."

"You mean – that?"

Funeral certainly did. He had been given a quart of whiskey for Christmas and he wanted to give the bottle to somebody who would appreciate it. Quinn, with his strong appetite for whiskey, was a fitting candidate, was he not?

"He sure qualifies, Funeral. He'll drink it whiskey, bottle, label and cork, he will."

"But first I have to find him."

"He hear about that free quart, and he'll come loping."

Funeral left. He had put out his bait. Word would reach old man Quinn and he would be pulled in by the magnet. Funeral went to the saloons. Nobody had seen Quinn recently. Had he bought a bottle of beer lately? Yes, he had bought a bottle, right before the fire, and he had said it had been for Old Press Johnson. He had left the saloon, bottle in hand.

Funeral frowned, and an alarm started to clang in him. It tolled with deep and insistent tones. He went into an alley and down it and came to a small frame shack that faced a pile of tin cans. He knocked on the door twice and knocked loudly. The thought came that old man Quinn might have passed out. The door was unlocked so he entered. He was in a small room. The room had the smell of unwashed clothing, of dirty piled-up bedding, of stale cooking.

But Quinn was not in his castle.

By now Funeral was openly worried. He stood there in the litter with the smell in his nostrils and he did some thinking. Then the thought came that his worry was with foundation. The old drunk was probably asleep in some alley or with some friend at the friend's house. He met Six Shooter Bob and asked him if he had seen the old drunk. This meeting occurred in the alley outside Quinn's house.

"Ain't seen him, Funeral. Kinda lookin' for the ol' rat myself."

"Was he at the fire?"

"Never seen him there. He's probably passed out somewhere. When he gets too drunk he beds down in the brush alongside the crick."

"But he hasn't had time to get drunk. He was sober when he went after the bottle of beer for Old Press Johnson."

"He's aroun' . . . somewhere."

"Maybe he fell dead somewhere full of booze," Funeral said at length. "Doc says the old souse had a weak heart."

A hand tugged at Funeral O'Neills sleeve and he looked down into the excited face of a boy about nine years old.

"Mr. O'Neill, there's no use lookin' for Ol' Man Quinn." Sonny Myers had evidently been running and he had to stop for breath. "We found him some other kids and me – down along the crock – in the brush – "

"Drunk, huh?"

"No, not drunk! He's — he's — dead!"

For the second time that day the fingers of Undertaker Funeral O'Neill explored the back of a dead man's skull. Old Man Quinn had gray hair, matted with sticks and debris. The skull moved in and out under the pressure of the mortician's long fingers. Then Funeral reared upward to his gaunt height. He stood there and looked down at the dead man.

"Dead," he intoned.

Ringbone Smith, chewing on a peppermint, looked up at his partner, his eyes forming a question.

"What's done killed him, Funeral?"

"He has been slugged from the back. He has been hit with a wide instrument could have been a sock full of sand. Anyway, it left a crushing, mauling effect — the entire back of his skull is fractured."

Sonny Myers stood close to Ringbone Smith. The boy had wide eyes and a white face. This was a day he would never forget. The wind strengthened suddenly, driving in the rain; the rain lashed across the earth in fierceness. It drove them under the branches of a wide Boxelder tree. Rain washed over the face of Quinn, but he, of course, did not know this.

This was indeed a puzzle. What enemy had disposed of this old drunk – this harmless old stiff? A cow bawled to her calf, somewhere in the thick buckbrush along the creek. They heard the calf answer his mother. Then there was only the wind and the rain.

"The rest of the danged town will be out here soon," Ringbone Smith grunted. "We had best look for tracks, huh?"

"No use."

"Why not?"

"This rain will have washed all tracks away. But we can look anyway before the thundering herd gets out here."

"Big day for Boxelder," Ringbone Smith murmured.

The body had been lying in a coulee. They had carried it out to higher ground. Evidently the old man had been thrown in the coulee. For you could clearly see where the body had tumbled down the bank, for the brush showed this – a pathway of bent and broken brush. But the wagon-road showed nothing. Some ruts, nothing more – ruts left by wagons and buggies and spring-wagons. Rain filled the ruts. Rain had washed away all boot tracks . . . if there had been any boot tracks.

Ringbone Smith summed it up. "Somebody might have slugged him downtown and then toted him out here in a wagon and dumped him into this coulee. These children just happened to stumble on his body by accident. Otherwise he would have laid here for days."

Funeral nodded. His partner had expressed a good strong point. But this led his thinking to another point. Who had murdered this old man – and for what reason? His mind went over possible reasons. Not for money, for Quinn had no money – he was an old stove-up cowboy, too old to hire out his saddle and lasso. Because of hate? Nobody could hate this old recluse enough to take his life.

"Maybe he just got too drunk," Ringbone said, "and he went off for a walk, and he slipped and fell down this bank, conking his head on one of them boulders on the way down?"

"Possible, but not probable."

Ringbone studied his partner. The cow again bawled for her calf. Evidently he was back in the brush and was bedded down in a place where the wind or rain could not hit him and he did not want to move. Again the rain moved in, slanting and cold, pushing against their slickers. Sonny Myers moved closer to Ringbone and his hand went up and found that of the veterinarian.

"Why do you say that, Shylock O'Neill?"

This time Funeral did not correct his friend, for he knew that Ringbone Smith knew the difference between Shylock and Sherlock, and he let it go at that. So he said, "You forget one thing."

"And that?"

"Old Press says that when he sent Quinn after the bottle of beer, Quinn was cold sober."

"Well, he could have fallen off that ledge, sober or drunk."

"He had no reason to be out walking in this god awful weather," the undertaker pointed out.

"Yeah, reckon you're right."

"Here comes some people," Sonny Myers said.

"The whole danged town," Ringbone said.

"Led by the county attorney," Funeral said quietly. "Never seen George Parnell out in such weather before. And beside that he's walking right fast, too."

"Hope he don't over exert his heart."

The group milled around. For the most part the citizens wore slickers and these were made of oilskin, either yellow or black. Rain helmets turned the rain. They stomped around like a herd of milling cattle. They asked questions and wondered and gawked and, for once, Old

Man Quinn was the center of the stage, although this honor had come somewhat late, Funeral thought wryly.

"He's dead, ain't he?" the county attorney asked.

"As a five year old boot," Ringbone Smith said.

Parnell had puzzled eyes. "Heart probably got an over jolt of whiskey." He looked at a man beside him. "You keep on drinking, Wilson, and that is the way you'll go, man."

"At least I'll go happy," Wilson said, and took a long drink.

Funeral asked. "Where is the doc?"

"He wouldn't come out in this rain," the attorney informed. "Said it might be hard on his ulcers. Just down right lazy. Been living off the public payroll too long. Dunlap is coming, but he is slower than molasses in January."

"Nobody has murdered this old stiff," a townsman said. "He's bashed out his brains on one of those rocks yonderly. He wouldn't harm a butterfly in a net, he's that peaceful."

"He *was* that peaceful," a man corrected.

Funeral turned away. "Leave the body lie there until the sheriff comes, if he can ever make it this far out of town. Then take him to my morgue."

"You'll fill your establishment yet," the county attorney joked. "Did you ever have a full house, Funeral?"

"Only in a poker game, and then darned few times." Funeral glanced significantly at Ringbone Smith. "No use old men standing here in this cold rain, veterinarian. Let's mosey, huh?"

"Sure thing."

Old Press Johnson was asking questions of the onlookers. Sonny Myers was now talking to the reporter-printer. Sonny and the other boys had been out hunting cottontails. They had stumbled over the body. They had gone hunting directly after the fire had been extinguished in the Tribune office. They had, in fact, been leaving town when the fire had broken out, but had run back to help put out the flames.

"Old Press sure will have a big edition,"

Funeral O'Neill said.

Ringbone plodded through mud, nodding agreement. "Two deaths, his editor in jail charged with murder, and a case of suspected arson almost taking the Tribune's headquarters. Looks to me, Funeral, like a female is barging down on us from the direction of Boxelder?"

"Looks like Millie Wetherford."

The girl turned out to indeed be young Ed Barnett's would-be wife. She had a bright face and despite the straight lines of her raincoat you could still see the promise of her womanhood.

She was full of questions. Who had killed Quinn? Had he died through an accident? These two could not, of course, be answered at this time. Yes, a deputy was stationed in front of Ed's cell, or else she would not be here. She hurried to where the townspeople were looking at Quinn and the partners sloshed their way into town, water seeping through their boots, the rain wetting their trousers below the hems of their raincoats.

They entered Funeral O'Neill's morgue

by the back door. This made them walk past the corpse of Colt Hagen on their way to the office proper. Funeral noted that Ringbone Smith did not want to look at the body. Hagen lay on the slab with his arms dangling over the sides and his mouth gaping open. He was not a lovely sight. Funeral decided to torment his partner.

"Look at this, Ringbone?"

Ringbone stopped, looked inquiringly at his partner. Orneriness tugged at the lanky undertaker and made him form a half-smile on his lips. He walked over and put his thumb hard against the dead man's wide nose. The imprint of his thumb did not rise in the flesh and It made a dent in the man's nose.

"What does that prove?" Ringbone asked testily.

"He's ready for the needle," Funeral joked.

Ringbone said nothing.

Funeral surveyed the corpse with a professional eye. "But he'll keep until morning. Cool back here. No flies, either."

Ringbone almost choked. "Let me out of here." He moved toward the office. When Funeral entered the vet was warming his back against the pot-bellied heater. There was a moment of silence. Rain dripped mournfully off the eaves. The wind made sounds in the overhang of the building.

Finally Ringbone spoke. "All right, Funeral, what do you say, friend?"

"I'd like your theories first, if you don't mind."

Ringbone Smith looked at his big knuckles. "All right, man – for what they are worth, if anything. I don't think they are worth much. Let's go to the beginning. Gardner wants to chouse out the hoemen. He had to silence Ed Burnett because the pen, after all, is mightier than the gun, like the poet fellow said."

"The sword, not the gun."

Ringbone waved his hand. "All right, corrected I stand, Funeral. Therefore I can see why Burnett and trouble meet head on and lock horns. But where in the heck does a harmless old drunk like Quinn come in at?"

"Suicide, maybe?"

Ringbone Smith snorted around his peppermint. The lines around his mouth grew hard and deep.

"A man can't commit suicide by hitting himself over the back of the skull with a club! He just can't do it, Funeral." Suddenly his mouth opened and the peppermint lay idle on his broad bovine tongue. A slow scheming look came into his dull eyes and gave them a somewhat flinty expression. "A club . . . ," he murmured, "a club . . . A club knocked Old Press Johnson cold, too. Knocked him into dream land. Funeral, is there some connection there?"

"There might be."

"I wonder . . . "

"But why would anybody club old Quinn to death?"

Funeral did not get to answer that question. A procession of men crossed in front of the window, out on the plank sidewalk, and a man hammered on the door.

"Let us in, Funeral."

"Funeral procession toting in Quinn's carcass," Ringbone Smith said.

Funeral hollered, "Open the door, fellow. It isn't locked."

The door was kicked unceremoniously open and about six men entered, four of them holding the corners of a canvas tarp. Suspended on this tarp, sagging as thought riding in a hammock, was the booze-beaten body of old man Quinn. He was half curled and he looked to all the world as though merely sleeping off a drunk.

"Where does you want him set down?" Sheriff Dunlap asked.

The question was a stupid one. Sheriff Dunlap knew full well where the undertaker's slab was there in the back room. Funeral had a touch of anger and this changed to disgust that colored his voice with bright sarcasm.

"Put him on the slab alongside of Colt Hagen," the lanky mortician said, "and then you crawl in between the two stiffs, Dunlap, and take a long peaceful nap, huh?"

"A joke," Dunlap said. "A joke."

A few of the men laughed. It was not funny. But long ago Funeral had given up trying to decipher the reason that men laughed. Some of them would laugh at anything, he knew.

They went through the door, a gang of muddy noisy men, and soon the pair heard a thud — this was Quinn's body landing on the slab. He was now lying on his back beside Colt Hagen.

Ringbone Smith smiled. "Seems to me, if my memory is correct, that Colt Hagen and old man Quinn hated each other right well, because Colt would never advance the old man any money for beer or whiskey?"

"He really hated Hagen."

"Now they are bed partners," the veterinarian said with a smile. "Which shows we never know what will happen to us."

"And good for us we don't."

Two of the makeshift pallbearers came back into the office and the others left by the back door. The two that returned to the office were County Attorney George Parnell and Sheriff Dunlap. The sheriff wore a deep and somewhat disturbed scowl that added not one iota to his ugliness.

"That ain't no way to talk to a man of my importance and public office, Funeral," the sheriff grumbled.

"Oh, hell," Funeral said, "I'm sorry."

The sheriff was mad and his face showed it. "I don't like to be pushed around," he warned.

Funeral said, "You got a lot of trouble to attend to Dunlap. You got to find out who murdered old man Quinn. You can't find out standing in my office and arguing with me."

The sheriff watched him, eyes bright bits of bead. "Well, all right," he said grudgingly. "Maybe I flew off the handle too fast."

"Sorry," Funeral said, but he didn't mean it. And the sheriff knew this. Sheriff Dunlap turned sharply and went out into the rain, leading the three of them in the office. County Attorney Parnell showed a thin smile. "He was really riled," the lawyer said.

"Good for him," Ringbone Smith grunted.

Funeral changed the subject. "Wonder *who* or *what* caved in the back of Quinn's head, and for *why* if it was murder?"

"He doesn't own a horse," Ringbone said.

"He owned two things," Funeral O'Neill said. "An empty pocketbook and a great appetite for alcohol in any shape or form. And if a horse had kicked him, we would have found the horse somewhere out in the brush or he'd have drifted back to town, it appears to me."

"This has me up a stump," Parnell said. "I guess we make that inquest tomorrow a double one, huh?"

"Might just as well," Funeral said. "Save time and the county's money."

Parnell said, "So long, men," and left. But Ringbone Smith and Funeral O'Neill were not alone long, for the doctor entered. He smelled of medicants and whiskey and his eyes were watery.

"I want to look at Quinn."

"He's dead," the undertaker said.

"I still want to see his corpse."

Funeral shrugged. "Back on the slab." He followed the medico into the room but Ringbone Smith remained with his back to the stove. The doctor jammed a rough hand against the dead man's mouth and got his jaw open. Then he got his bottle out of his hip pocket, pulled out the cork with his teeth, and poured a snort down the man's throat. He grinned like a monkey who had stolen a banana off a fruit-cart.

"My old friend, Quinn," the man of medicine intoned. "Happy drinking on the other side, you old soak." He looked at Funeral. "I knew his background well; over many a bottle of cribbage game . . . He has no known relatives. Shoot him full of formalin and plant him deep and send me the bill."

Funeral nodded.

"I loved the old stiff."

"You're drunk," the undertaker said.

The doctor looked at the open cavern that was Quinn's mouth. "Terrible way for a man of his drinking ability to die."

"Why say that?"

"Here he practiced for years trying to drink himself to death. Then he gets tricked and either gets bounced over the head or falls and slaps his coconut against a boulder. And our great sheriff – he is helpless and, beside that, he has sawdust for brains. There is an election coming up, you know. And the blessed voters – they might elect a new sheriff, Dunlap." He caught himself and hiccupped. "God bless the voters. They always seem to elect the dumbbells. Is that because only stupid men run for office, Funeral?"

"You got me," Funeral said, and grinned.

The medico pivoted on one heel. He let loose a savage rebel yell. "Hurry for Jeff Davis!" He stumbled across the office, opened the door, and stepped out into the rain.

Ringbone Smith, hands behind, moved over to the window. His smile was wide. "He fell off the sidewalk into the mud face down. Now he is trying to get up. The sin of drink, Funeral."

"Without it," said Funeral, "the world would be dead."

"He the root of all evil," the undertaker intoned. "Now he has at last gathered his feet under him and he is wobbling down the street toward the saloon. What would his professors in medical school say about their top student now, I wonder?"

"Get your hat," Funeral said, "and we'll go over to the jail."

They went down the street – gaunt and tall Funeral O'Neill and short and squat Ringbone Smith – an undertaker and a veterinarian – and the dusk was creeping in, sneaking through the rain, touching the corners of the buildings, settling against and claiming the soaked soil. The wind had died down somewhat. What wind there was had a high cold chill. The rain would do much good. Crops would be revived, for wheat and oats were starting to form heads; this rain would fill out those heads, making for round firm kernels. Corn would also like this rain. Grass would grow on the benchlands, and cattle would graze. Farmers and cowmen alike would profit by Nature's extravagance.

Lamps had come into yellow life, glowing in the windows of stores and other business establishments. The thought came to Funeral O'Neill that this probably was the most exciting day Boxelder, Montana, had ever experienced in its short but hectic life. The events of this day, tragic and stirring, would provide fuel for conversation for many, many years. But then he switched his mind over to the problem at hand. He had been instrumental in getting young Ed Burnett to Boxelder to take over the Tribune. Therefore, in a measure, he was responsible for the young newspaperman's present and future safety.

They went down the cell corridor, the yellow bracket-lamps spreading their light, making shadows run ahead of them, become even with them, then go behind them. Ed Burnett had a lamp lighted in his cell. He was playing cards with his deputy. Millie Wetherford loafed on the bunk, watching the game. Funeral O'Neill smiled. Jail was not too tough on young Ed.

Ed said, "Howdy, men. Comer on in, the door is unlocked. Yes, I heard all about old man Quinn's passing. I reckon he got killed, but I don't know why. Who killed him?"

"Sheriff Dunlap will find the murderer," Funeral said.

"Dunlap – find the murderer – He couldn't find the bottom of his right foot in the dark." Ed Burnett then saw the undertaker's smile. "Why was he killed?"

"Once a newshawk, always a newshawk," Ringbone Smith said slowly. "Even behind bars a prisoner – he asks questions for a story."

Funeral glanced at the deputy, whom he had known for years. "Want to watch him, Carl. He'll talk you into lending him your gun and you taking his place here."

"We're old friends," the deputy said, playing a card. "He's an old riddle I finally solved. You keep your mind on your cards, Burnett, or I'll play pinochile with Millie, whose face is much nicer to look at across a table."

Ed grinned and played a card. "I got to get out of here, men," he said, looking up at Funeral and his partner.

"Due process of law," Funeral said. "You have long advocated this in your press. Be sure, young man, you abide by this theory."

"Thanks, Grandpa," Ed said, in feigned cynicism. But I should write this story up. Old Press is no hand with a pencil. He can't even spell right. But, reckon there is nothing to do but wait."

"Right," Ringbone Smith said.

Funeral O'Neill said, "Ringbone and I will go over and help Old Press."

Ed Burnett snorted. "You two help . . . That's a laugh. You don't even know type lice when you see them!"

"Thanks," Funeral said.

Ed said, "I could write the stories if I had the facts. Maybe you better send Old Press over to talk with me. I can get the information from him and write the stories here in my cell."

"We might do that," Funeral said. "What opinions do you have on this Quinn murder, Ed?"

Ed glanced up at the undertaker. "I know one thing. I never murdered him. It happened when I was safe in jail. Had I been out Clint Gardner by hook or crook would have tried to pin something on me, just to be ornery." He played a card. "Wonder if that skunk of a Gardner had anything to do with it?"

"Why ask that?" Funeral asked.

"He's in everything rotten, right to his neck. I can't see any motivation for anybody wanting to kill old man Quinn, but there's a lot here I can't understand, and what I don't understand I lay onto Clint Gardner, because he'd lay it onto me just as fast."

The deputy was a law-abiding man so

he said, "No more of that talk, please, Ed. You can't prove anything like that so why say it, friend? Play your cards and forgit ol' Quinn because it is up to the law to find his killer, if he was killed. He might have fell and bashed in his head."

"Probable, but almost impossible," Ed Burnett said sourly. He winked at Funeral and Ringbone. "Sure will be a rotten edition with you two slaving over a galleys."

"Thanks again," Funeral said.

Ringbone Smith found himself glancing up at his tall partner but Funeral O'Neill did not meet his eyes. The veterinarian could see no purpose in this visit or in this bantering talk. Funeral seemed to be debating about something. Ringbone Smith, who knew him well, wondered what thoughts troubled his companion. He had one theory tucked away back in his mind. But he had not given it tongue as yet. He was a patient man, and his mental processes, although they moved and matured slowly, were thorough and fine of teeth and detail. What he made in slowness he made up for in thoroughness. Accordingly he waited for Funeral O'Neill to make the first move.

The deputy scowled, studied his cards, and then asked, "Wonder if there are any strangers in town, men?"

"Wonder if there are any strangers in town, men?"

Funeral nodded. Apparently he had had the same question in his mind and had found its answer.

"Only stranger in town that I know of is that pink-faced dude who stays at the hotel. Thet gent who is so wide across the seat of his pants, Carl. He came into town about a week ago, I reckon." The undertaker directed his next question to Publisher Ed Burnett. "What is that man's name, Ed?"

"I don't know. I don't even know who you mean."

Funeral grunted, "Heck of a newspaperman. No wonder the column on *local items* is so short and incomplete. You know what I mean. I saw you talking to him a while back, couple of days ago."

"Oh, that fellow!" Ed played a card but did not look up. "Don't remember his name, and I did put it in local items – the day or so after he hailed into town. Your play, Carl."

Ringbone Smith had had enough. "Let's get out of here," he said.

They went toward the Town Cafe. Neither man spoke. The rain came in, falling slanting against them, and water dripped off eave-troughs. Darkness was almost complete now. This would be a good night to sit beside the fire and read a magazine. Or else just sit and doze.

They went into a booth. The waitress came with the utensils. Ringbone jabbed a fork toward a portly man sitting toward the front of the cafe. They had walked past him on their way to the booth.

"That the gent you mean, Funeral?"

Funeral glanced at the man. His wide bottom covered the stool very convincingly. He had a big belly that sagged over his belt. He had a wide and heavy face with hanging jowls. His face was almost cherubic-looking.

"Didn't your mother ever teach you not to point, Ringbone?" Funeral O'Neill spoke softly. "Yes, that is the man to whom I referred while talking to the deputy and Ed Burnett and Millie."

"What is his handle?"

"According to what he signed in the hotel register, his name is Michael Henderson. His home town is listed as being back East."

"You snoop around worse than Old lady Freeman."

"Thank you, sir."

"Now why are we a-wastin' our time talking about this stranger?"

"No apparent reason. You started it, remember."

"We'd best get outside our vittles and get over to the Tribune Office and get to work with Old Press, because that deadline is roaring down on us."

"I don't think we will be much help."

"Neither do I, to be honest . . . for once."

They got their meal and ate, taking their time. Rain washed off the roof. Everybody talked about the rain, about Ed Burnett, about Colt Hagen, or about Quinn. They had to go past Henderson to get to the cash box. Funeral noticed in the long back mirror that Henderson gave them a quick — although complete — glance. This done, he looked at them again; he did not notice that Funeral had caught his glance in the mirror.

Funeral followed his partner outside. The second glance given to them by the man called Henderson had been critical and evaluating, Funeral had been quick to notice. It had definitely not been the casual type of glance a man puts upon a man in whom he has no pressing interest. Or was he reading something into the study given them by the heavy set stranger?

"Now we become printers," Ringbone said. He belched like a hog linging up at corn trough. "And what a newspaper this next one will be, huh!"

"Should really be something," Funeral said.

The lamp was lit in the Tribune's office. But the blinds were pulled low. Funeral tried the knob but the door was locked. That, he figured, was only logical – Old Press Johnson had been slugged once, and he was leaving no more doors unlocked. The undertaker hammered on the door but got no response.

"Old Press sure can hear that, even if he is back in the composing room," Ringbone Smith grunted. He cocked his head. "I can't hear no press running, and that old press makes the town rumble, it's so noisy."

"I'll try the window."

"The window might be bolted down," Ringbone said. "You know, I'm worried."

"Oh, you're an old woman."

The window rose slowly, for rain had swollen it shut. But Funeral got his leg inside and got into the room. He was in the office. The door leading to the composing room was closed.

He unlatched the front door and let his partner enter. Then, with Ringbone behind him, he opened the door leading to the workshop. The lamps were lit. One hung from the wall. Another stood on a desk. The back door was open, Funeral noticed; the thought came that they should have gone to the back. Old Press was not around.

Ringbone said, "Maybe he just stepped out, forgettin' to shut the door. Hey, Funeral, look!"

He pointed at a shadow beside the desk. His lips trembled; his voice was a rough whisper.

Funeral moved over and looked down at the Negro, who lay there full length on the floor. Old Press lay on his belly with both arms flung out, his feet close together. The thought came that this was the second time this day that he had seen the Negro lying prone on this floor.

"Somebody has killed him!" Ringbone Smith said huskily.

Funeral asked, "How do you know he is dead?" but he did not wait for an answer. He ran across the room, pistol in his hand, and he ran out the open back door. He was in the alley. Rain roared down, savage and intense, driving against him, a million invisible small hands hammering on him. The alley had a little light from the back of an establishment. Into this light hurried a man, his back to Funeral. The man was about thirty feet away. He was walking fast, almost running. Funeral cried out, "Wait a minute," and he hit the man just as the man turned. He tackled him from behind, doubling the man's knees.

Because of the darkness, the undertaker could not identify the man. The man had been turning when Funeral had tackled him. The undertaker went forward, sliding into the rain; he made a good hard tackle. It would have done credit to a halfback. He heard the man grunt, half in surprise and half with shock. The man's head snapped back, he sagged ahead, and when he came down his head hit a heavy steel garbage pail.

Funeral went past him, turned, and

was on him instantly. But, strangely, the man put up no struggle; he was limp and harmless there in the mud. Only then did the undertaker realize the blow had knocked the man unconscious. He had really hit that heavy pail. And Funeral had also hit him very, very hard. The attack had been unexpected. The man had been loose of muscle.

The garbage can had been full of vegetable trimmings. The man lay on his belly. Across his back he had a bouquet of lettuce leaves. These the undertaker knocked to one side and he rolled the man over so he could see his face.

Although the light was not very powerful, he indentified the man. He got to his feet and said, "Well, I'll be dog-goned," and he walked back to the door of the printing-shop, knocking mud from his slicker. He figured the man had not seen him clearly enough to recognize him.

Apparently nobody had heard the ruckus for nobody came into the alley to investigate. At this point Ringbone

Smith came to the back door of the print-shop, the lamplight outlining his wide body.

"Where are you?" he asked.

"Right here."

"Couldn't see you in that dark. Did I hear you holler at somebody a while back?"

"Not me," Funeral lied.

"Why did you go in the alley?"

"To see if anybody was loitering around."

"See anybody?"

"Not a soul," Funeral lied again. Evidently Ringbone could not see the unconscious man because of the darkness.

"Old Press ain't dead," the veterinarian said.

Funeral growled, "You should check to make sure before you holler anything like you did yelp, about him being dead."

"I got excited, I reckon."

"What's the matter with him?"

They went to where the Negro still lay on the floor.

"He's drunk," Ringbone Smith said.

Funeral studied his partner. "He can't be dead drunk. He was sober just a few minutes back. A man can't get dead drunk and unconscious in just a half hour or so. Isn't logical."

"But he is out cold."

Funeral O'Neill went to his knees beside the recumbent printer. He leaned forward and smelled the Ned's breath. It stunk. He sniffed, hating the smell; some of it was whiskey, and some of the stink smelled like varnish. He brushed some more and from his slicker. "Fell over a danged cat out in the alley," he explained.

"Black?"

"Blue," he joked.

"Let's get him sitting up, huh, Funeral?"

Funeral and his partner got Old Press with his back against a bench. But this made no difference in the Negro. He was out cold. His big head lopped over and his lips rattled in loose unison as he snored. But he remained sitting, for his shoulder was wedged against the leg of the table.

"His breath smells like a distillery," Ringbone said. "It would take the paint off a paint horse, hair and all."

Funeral sniffed again. "He smells terrible. He must be doped. I wonder if he takes any dope? Did you ever hear about him having any heart trouble?"

"Only with that little colored gal who use to work in the cafe – the one that ran off with that big Texas colored cowboy."

"You sure have an odd sense of humor," Funeral said dryly.

Funeral O'Neill then slapped Old Press across the jowls. His blows moved the man's head but his eyes did not open. Funeral slapped him three times and then stood up, frowning in perplexity.

"He sure is out cold, and no maybe about it."

Ringbone looked at a bottle on the bench. The cork was out of it. "He must've been drinkin' out of that quart," the veterinarian said. "Just about one drink taken out of it, too. New quart, looks like to me."

"Been opened before," Funeral said.

"How do you know?"

Funeral pointed out that the quart of whiskey had once been sealed. But no seal or remnants of the seal were around, either on the bench or in the wastepaper basket. "So somebody must have broke the seal before tonight," he reminded.

"Right . . . if it means anything, which it might not."

"I'd say, off hand, that he is doped – and doped good," the funeral director said. "And the whiskey in that bottle has knocked him unconscious." He leaned over and smelled of the bottle's neck. "This smells like whiskey, but it still has some of that stink in it that is in Old Press."

"That bottle has come out of Ed Burnett's desk," Ringbone said, eyes narrowed. "I'm sure that is Ed's desk."

"That's where he works."

Ringbone Smith crammed a red peppermint between his teeth. He spoke around it with cold clarity.

"Somebody might have poisoned that whiskey. Figure Ed Burnett would drink it. 'Stead of that, Old Press tied into it."

"Could be so."

Ringbone tasted of the whiskey, grimaced, then spat it out. "Tastes just like whiskey to me, and I hardly ever taste it. Rotten stuff."

"Sure is," Funeral said, and grinned.

The veterinarian put the bottle back on the desk. "This is getting deeper and deeper every minute, Funeral. Seems to me this is too serious a thing to be tied in with something as small as homesteads and farmers – and a man writing an editorial. This is maybe attempted murder?"

"Could be."

"Something else is behind this," the vet said. "Here comes somebody – in the back door – on the run, sounds like."

A man barged in the back door. He was round and his moon-like face showed excitement. This excitement rimmed his words, also, giving them a high-pitched alarm. The man was Michael Henderson.

"Hey, there's a man laying out there in the alley. He's either dead or unconscious – I stumbled on him . . . almost fell."

Funeral O'Neill studied the man. "What the hell were you doing out in the alley?" he asked. "The sidewalks are in front of the buildings in this town, not behind them. And what are you talking about? Are you drunk, stranger?"

"I'm not drunk. I almost fell over him. He's out there – by a garbage can – He might be sick. He groaned like he was ailing."

"I'll light the lantern," Ringbone Smith said.

He took the kerosene lantern off the hook and lit it and they went into the rain, the rays of the lantern making their legs look like giant scissors by throwing the shadows against the wet earth and water-soaked building. When they arrived, the man was sitting up, rain and mud in his face. Despite its dull rays the lantern showed his wild eyes.

"Shucks," Ringbone said, "Gittler, the farmer that is head of the Grangers. What the heck you doing here sittin' in this mud, Gittler?"

Gittler said, huskily, "That's what I'd like to know. Help me to my pins, men? Lord, my head aches – fit to bust. What the hell happened to me, I wonder?"

Funeral O'Neill almost sighed out loud, he was so relieved. This farmer, then, had not recognized him – that was good! He and Henderson got the farmer between them and, with Ringbone and the lantern in the lead, they got Gittler into the press room, where he sank into a chair and held his head between his hands, head down in pain.

Funeral spoke to Henderson. "Better go down and get the doc. That is, if he hasn't passed out, too. You know where his office is, don't you?"

"I know."

Henderson waddled out, going by the front door.

Then both the partners stood there and looked at Fred Gittler. Old Press slept, jammed against the desk. From outside came the crash of thunder.

Then lightning was bright again, washing across the ranges, and more thunder sounded.

"Wild night," Ringbone said.

"Yes, and in more ways than one."

Gittler looked up then. His eyes had become steady now. He fixed them on Funeral, then moved his gaze over to Ringbone.

"Thanks for the help, men."

Funeral said, "Glad to help you, Gittler. I reckon you took one drink too many, huh?"

"No, not that. I don't know what happened."

Funeral scowled deeply. He glanced at Ringbone Smith, who watched in silence. Then the undertaker swung his sunken eyes back to the farmer.

"I don't understand that statement."

Gittler said, "I was walking along. Seems to me somebody hollered, and I went to turn – Something or somebody hit me from behind."

"Across the head?" asked Ringbone.

"No, around the waist – mebbe the knees. I went surging ahead, and then I never knew anything until you men came out with that lantern. Who found me?"

"That newcomer," Funeral said.

"Oh, Michael Henderson, huh?"

"I reckon that is his name," Funeral said.

Now Gittler, for the first time, saw Old Press. His mouth opened almost as wide as that of the Negro and a look of fear came across his face. "He's – he's dead – ?"

"No, not dead," Funeral said.

"What's the matter – with him?"

"Drunk," Ringbone Smith supplied.

Gittler said, "The old soak. Ain't he got enough trouble in life without adding onto it come tomorrow with a hangover. Oh, my head."

"You got a hangover without drinking

I'd say," Funeral said, and grinned. He was glad Gittler had not identified him. But what reason had the man to be back there in the alley. No more reason than had Michael Henderson.

Gittler looked up. "If I shook my head my brains would rattle like dried peas in a pod." He looked again at Old Press' gaping mouth. "He sure got stiff fast. He was cold sober when he was down where the kids found Quinn dead. He was asking questions and scribbling on a pad, even in the rain."

Ringbone merely nodded. Funeral said, "Sure must have hit him lightning fast."

Gittler got uncertainly to his feet. Evidently his knees were made of water. He caught the desk, steadied himself, and shook his head gingerly. Then a look of anger crossed his stern face.

"Somebody must have tackled me. If I knew who he was I'd twist the son into a pretzel and eat him with no salt on, cooked or raw. I'm thankful to you men, and maybe someday I can return the favor?"

"The doc is prob'ly coming to look at you," Ringbone said. "So sit down again, farmer, and rest?"

"Got to keep moving, but thanks."

Gittler lurched out the back door, and disappeared in the storm. Ringbone moved back and closed the door and looked at Funeral O'Neill with a smug smile on his face. His glance was one of casual curiosity.

"I don't reckon you know anything about this, Funeral?"

"Not a thing."

"Seems to me I seen you knock some mud off your slicker a while back, when you come back from the alley."

"You saw wrong."

Ringbone Smith grinned, moved forward, boots creaking with water and mud. He looked down at Old Press Johnson, who was still deep in Morpheus' arms.

"I wonder," he murmured, "I wonder."

Funeral had no question. He was still thinking of Fred Gittler. Gittler had no reason to be going down a sloppy, slippery alley when the main street had high and sure plank sidewalks. And then he remembered that Michael Henderson had not given him an answer to his question about what he, a stranger, was doing in an alley? Somewhere there was a key to this whole thing. This key would unlock this entire affair and throw open a door that showed clarity. But, as yet, the undertaker had not found that key — would he find it, he wondered?

To get to his hotel, Henderson did not have to walk through an alley. All he had had to do was leave the cafe, move a few buildings down the sidewalk, and come to his cafe. This was the most logical and the shortest distance from the cafe to the hotel. And in a night as wild as this one, a man did not go for a pleasure walk down a dark alley.

He turned his attention to Ringbone Smith.

Ringbone had dipped a bucketful of water out of the barrel behind the shop. He had a sponge and he had filled this with water. Now he was compressing the sponge and letting water trickle down on Old Press' kinky gray-black hair.

"He sure don't seem to cotton to snap out of it, Funeral."

"How is his heart action?"

Funeral's fingers found the man's throat. He kept his head down as he counted aloud.

"Sounds about right to me," Funeral said.

Ringbone said, "Here comes a couple of men through the front office. Must be the doc and Henderson."

He proved to be correct. The doctor staggered a little and he almost fell to his knees beside the black man. The doctor sent an evil glance up at Funeral O'Neill.

"What do you want me to do?"

"Bring him out of it, of course."

"Well, well, how simple." The drunken medico turned his drunken attention onto the drunken man. "I'll be like him in a little while. One or two dozen more shots of bourbon, Old Press, and I'll be with you." He felt the man's pulse, rolled his head back, lifted an eyelid, let it fall. "His eyes are still in him," he said. "Big as billiard balls. Did one of them have the number 9 on it?"

"Number 11," Funeral said.

Ringbone Smith was disgusted, but he said nothing. Michael Henderson watched in what was apparent amusement.

The doctor reached out and snagged his bag. He got out a hypodermic syringe and a bottle and he inserted the needle through the cap. He filled the hypo with about twenty c.c.s. of the bottle's contents. Then he spoke to Michael Henderson, and his needle was poised over Old Press' dark forearm.

"Get down on your knees, Henderson, and help me."

"Why?"

"He might come out of this in a fighting mood. You're as wide as a barn door. Just lie on him if he comes out wild."

"Sure," Henderson said, and smiled and went to his knees beside the printer. The doc plunged the needle into the skin and shot the solution into a vein. "Hit it on the line," he mumbled.

Ringbone Smith chewed and watched with fascination. He was so intent on watching the doctor that he did not hear Funeral O'Neill leave. Funeral had backed away as silently as he could, letting the stern attraction of the moment take the attention away from his departure.

Ringbone Smith glanced around in surprise, acting as though his partner had been dissolved into thin air. He sloshed his way to the back door and looked into the darkness of the alley but could not see his partner. He frowned in perplexity. But he knew Funeral had had some mission in mind. Accordingly he dismissed this from his thoughts and returned to the doctor and Henderson and Old Press.

As for Funeral O'Neill, he went down the alley, came to the end, circled around and, when he passed the cafe, he glanced inside. Fred Gittler sat on a stool sipping some hot coffee. The sight of the farmer again brought to his mind the problem that had confronted him that afternoon. Was Fred Gittler a Gardner spy, placed among the farmers?

He played with this thought. Then he discarded it. Time would reveal much, he was sure.

He went through the space between the hotel and the next building, squirming through in the dark, rain not hitting him here. When he came again to freedom he was in the alley behind the hotel. The hotel was two stories high, the only two-story building in town. An outside stairway ran up to the door that opened the upstairs halls. He took this stairway.

The stairway was not too strong. He thought he felt it sway under his weight. But he doubted that. The wind was blowing hard and it might have given him the effect of weakness in the stairs, for the wind swayed him with its force. He came to the upstairs door. He tried the knob. The knob turned but the door would not open. He stood there and thought, Bolted, from inside.

He stood there and gave this situation a brief but deep bit of exploratory thought. He wanted to get into the hotel. He wanted to get inside without anybody knowing. He stood there and thought. Rain dropped from leaden skies, the darkness was thick, and rain talked as it ran down the water-trough, tumbling from the end of the trough down the pipe to the over-flowing barrel, down below the ground. Suddenly he wished it would stop raining. He wished that with all his power. But wishes, he knew, were useless: action was what counted. If wishes were real, all beggars would ride. He pushed against the door again, but it held. It was bolted securely. The bolt was evidently above the knob.

Suddenly from down the alley below came a canine racket. Some dogs had tipped over the garbage can back of the cafe. They fought and snarled and the air was filled with snarling and rain.

Then the back door of the cafe broke open to throw a square of light across the alley. The dogs, for one moment, were pinpointed in this – they were fierce dark mongrels, fangs showing. From his porch Funeral could see them clearly. They stood there in terrible outline, fangs bared; one dog was down, another frozen over him. There was this tableau, grim and deadly, and then it broke, for the dogs moved in terror. They turned, their quarrel forgotten, and they fled; the perimeter of darkness moved in, claiming them. A man came out of the cafe and straightened the garbage can and put on the lid, jamming it down with finality. He wore a blue shirt and dark pants and a long white apron. He was mad and his profanity ruined the sweetness of the rain.

Then he returned to his cook-stove kingdom, shutting the door. And there was only the rain, and the wind. Funeral looked up and down the alley but saw nothing. Boxelder had had a rough – a very rough – day. Now the town and its people, for the most part, were resting.

His attention was again concentrated on the locked door.

His luck had run muddy. Should he go back down the creaky stairway, go to the front of the hotel, and enter through the lobby? He discarded this plan immediately. Usually the lobby had a few people playing whist with the proprietor. Or, if the card players were not present, then there was the clerk behind the counter. The clerk would greet him and ask why he was going upstairs, for he had no business in this hotel. He wanted to keep this expedition a secret.

Again he laid his weight against the door. It held and then sagged in slightly, for it was loose in its frame. With cold wet fingers he fumbled under the raincoat and got his pocketknife out of his pocket.

He got the long blade open. There in the dark he got the blade inserted between the door-stop – a strip of wood – and the jamb.

Despite the noise of the falling rain, he heard the steel of the knife collide with the steel of the bolt that held the door locked. He worked as quickly as he could. He had to push back the bolt a little bit at a time. His only hope was that the bolt handle, inside the door, would not fall into a notch; if this happened, the bolt would be wedged and locked, and he could do nothing. This did not happen, though. Slowly the blade slid back the bolt. Then suddenly, without warning, the door opened inwardly; elation filled him as he stepped into the lamplighted hallway.

Slowly he closed the door behind him. He shut out the sound of the rain and the howl of the wind.

He stood alone in the hall. A boot-worn carpet, scuffed and thin from years of bootheels, was on the floor. Doors were on each side of the hallway.

Kerosene lamps hung on the wall in bracket holders. They were old lamps of native copper which had not been polished for years and they were green and dirty. But he had no time to spend on the hotel fixtures. He had a job to do and he had best do it fast; time was the essence of this affair.

He moved ahead as silently as he could. From the stairway leading down to the lobby came the sounds of voices, both of men and women. The card game was in progress. He recognized voices, for he knew almost every soul in this cowtown. He reached the point where the stairway up from the lobby joined the hallway. He wondered if he could be seen from the lobby as he crossed this strip which was about three feet wide.

He darted across the strip. Evidently nobody had seen him for he heard no alarm in the voices below him; they had continued in their even tenor. He hoped none of the doors would suddenly open. None did. He came to the door that had the number 14 on its panel.

He tried the knob. This door also was locked. He called his pocket-knife again into action. He inserted it between the strips of wood and went to work. This door seemed even more difficult than the outer door. Minutes became hours and centuries bore down on him; actually, he opened the door in but a few minutes. Finally this door also swung in. It went in with its hinges voicing an oiless protest, the sound sharp in the hallway. Funeral slipped into the room. A lamp burned on the dresser, the wick turned low, the chimney dark with streaks of soot. He closed the door behind him and relocked it with a key lying on the dresser. He did not leave the key in the lock, though.

The room was small. The bed had a sagging spring and it was swayback as an old work horse. Plainly it had seen better days. There were two chairs, both somewhat the worse for wear, and a writing table against the far wall, level with the dresser. Two big suitcases, strapped together, were on the floor.

Funeral wasted no time; he went right to work. First he ransacked the bureau quickly. He found some men's shirts, some underwear, and other items of wearing apparel. He found a letter. But it was of no importance — it was from a woman — evidently the wife or sweetheart of the room's occupants. He glanced at it, saw it was of no value, then restored it to its resting place. It was useless to his cause. Next he turned his attention to the two tightly strapped suitcases. They were unlocked. The fact that their locks were not snaps showed him they held not what he was looking for; they would hold nothing of importance, or they would have been locked. Nevertheless he hurriedly ransacked through their contents. He found more shirts, handkerchiefs, a few pairs of pants, and some socks. He found not a bit of paper of any sort. He snapped them shut again and strapped them solidly and then stood there and did some thinking.

His eyes roamed the room searching out possible hiding-places for vital information. Perhaps he had gone off on a wrong tangent? He was working on premise, nothing more. Then he remembered Ed Burnett, there in jail. And he remembered that Ed had a murder charge hanging over his young head.

He looked at the bed. He looked at the sagging mattress. He walked over and lifted the edge of that mattress and ran his hand between it and the springs. His hand met some paper. He took out two letters. He read them slowly and deliberately, despite the pushing impact of the minute hand. He stored their contents in his brain, making his memory digest the words.

Then, carefully he replaced the letters in their original hiding place. He had just tidied up the mattress, getting it into its original swayback position, when he heard boots in the hall – boots moving toward Room 14. Quickly his gnarled hands smoothed out the faded pink bedspread. He heard boots stop outside the door. He heard knuckles lift, fall, on the panel. He heard a voice call a low name.

He knew that voice.

He stood back of the door and his Colt .45 was in his hand, raised shoulder high.

He waited, debating about unlocking the door, wondering if the man on the other side had a key.

"Come in," he said, hiding his identity behind a forced voice.

"Unlock the door."

"You got a key, ain't you?" Again, forced tones.

"Gettin' too lazy to open the door, huh?"

"In bed."

A key went into the lock. He heard steel grate on steel. The door opened and a man came in. He looked at the bed and said, "What the hell is this – ?" but he never got to finish his sentence.

He started to whirl, too.

He did not turn. The .45 saw to that. It came down with a sickening crunch. The barrel hit the man across the head. He never saw what hit him, nor did he see who had hit him. He didn't have time to grunt. His knees were shoved out ahead of him. He turned slightly, and then the floor came up and claimed him.

He fell on his face.

Funeral O'Neill breathed deeply, a deep sigh of thoughtfulness. He lifted his .45 and kissed the cold barrel and pouched it and grinned satanically. For the second time within an hour he had knocked cold two men. One by a flying tackle, the other by his .45.

He rolled the man over.

He studied the man's features, and his own face was grim and deadly. Then he arose to his gaunt savage height, his mind rummaging the dark corners of this problem. He found nothing of pressing importance, so he turned and went outside. He shut the door behind him. He went down the hall and met nobody and went down the back stairway into the rain and the wind. He moved down the alley, boots in mud; the wind drove his slicker tight against him outlining his gauntness. His mind was busy. He had gained some information. This was beginning to tie into itself, one thing overlacing the other, another thing coming in, weaving in, twisting in — this was building body and fabric, and these would make the whole. He was sure of that. He slid and almost fell; he found himself cursing the wind and the rain. He caught himself in time. His nerves were not steady; this trouble was a heavy weight — his nerves were sagging. They were, in a measure, like the old bed, back there in the hotel room. He thought of the man lying there on the floor.

Then he entered the back door of the Tribune's workshop.

Michael Henderson had left. With Old Press Johnson was the doctor and Ringbone Smith.

Funeral glanced at the printer. He had apparently just snapped out of it, but his eyes were glazed and glassy. The doctor was cursing him. He used a strange language. Funeral recognized it as Latin. He had studied a little Latin in mortician school, and he recognized curses when he heard them.

"Why cuss at him, doc?"

"He ain't coming to fast enough."

"You want to get back to your office and your bottle, huh?"

"How did you guess it?" The doctor was cynical.

Ringbone Smith turned appraisive eyes on his printer. "You come and go as silent as the wind. Where you been, son?"

"Ducked out to buy some eating tobacco."

"The store is closed at this hour, and the saloon only handles Old Briar, and you chew Horseshoe."

"I got some out of my establishment."

"Took you a long time."

"I'm a slow man," Funeral O'Neill said. "I'm getting old. My legs move slower. The night is a bad one. Wind and rain and hard to navigate. Any more orders, Ringbone?"

"Yes, keep your mouth shut."

"Gladly, if you do likewise."

Funeral returned his gaze to Old Press. He found himself remembering the man he had knocked cold there in the hotel room. He smiled against his will and Ringbone asked, "What's so funny?"

"You are," Funeral said.

"Thanks, chum."

Finally Old Press Johnson got to his feet with their aid. He stumbled over to a chair, found it with difficulty, and sat down, lowering his head into his ink-dark hands with their big knuckles and long fingers. Finally he looked up and in the lamplight his eyes were as big as billiard balls.

"What in the name of heaven all happened to this boy?" he asked the world in general. His eyes swiveled in damp sockets as they moved from man to man. "Did some hoodlum done knock me cold again, men?"

"You took a drink out of that bottle over there, remember?" Funeral said.

The billiard balls turned toward the whiskey bottle on the table. Remembrance apparently washed across the tortured brain. The thick lips moved and at first no words would come and then the words sprang free.

"Shore, now I remembers."

The gangling Negro got with difficulty to his feet and then sank back again, unable to stand up.

"I took one drink," he said, "and then the ceiling done caved in and hit me *smacko* and then the floor started to dance. I thought it was an earthquake at first, and then right afore I slips into the arms of Morpheus, I blamed it on the whiskey."

"Sure knocked you cold," Ringbone said. He told about how he and his partner had found the printer.

"I thank you, boys."

The doctor snapped shut his bag with professional smoothness. "My fee," he said, "is ten bucks, payable at this moment – here and now."

"Mail me the bill the first of the month," the Negro said.

"I want ten bucks, right now."

"Ain't you got no professional ethics, Doc?"

"I have oceans of ethics, but I have very little money. My throat aches for a slug of Old Saddle."

"I'll mail you the money."

"I want it now." The doctor looked

at Funeral and Ringbone. "I have had a busy, busy day. Somebody is going to pay me ten bucks. Quinn's work is on me – gratis – but I've doctored this printer two times today, and I want my pay."

"I'll pay you on the first, Doc."

"I don't trust you."

Old Press grinned. "At least, you are blunt." He dug in his right-hand pant's pocket. He came out with two gold pieces. He took the bigger one and handed it to the doctor. "You going to bite into it to see if it is good?" He was dripping sarcasm.

"Thanks, Old Press."

"Hope the first drink chokes you to death, Doc, like the first drink out of that bottle choked me and knocked me cold." The Negro frowned, huge ridges in his forehead. "That couldn't have been the first drink out of that bottle, 'cause the seal was done busted."

The doctor left, leaving behind him a smell of whiskey, iodine, and other sharp odors of his profession. This left the three of them – Funeral O'Neill, Ringbone Smith, and Old Press. And outside the wind continued to blow and the rain continued to fall. Funeral thought, one thing sure about Montana . . . when the rain starts, it never has sense enough to stop . . .

"Just one slug outa that bottle," Old Press moaned, "and I wobbles like a hen that has done swallered a lighted firecracker on the fourth of July. Then the firecracker explodes and I goes for a free ride across the stars. Man, what is in that likker, anyway?"

"Must be doped," Funeral said.

Old Press watched him. "You mean it came doped from the saloon where Ed bought it, Funeral?"

Funeral shook his head. "The seal was broken, you said. Somebody might have sneaked in and doped it."

"They'd have plenty of chance," the printer said. "The place is empty sometimes, with the doors open. But why dope it?"

"I don't think it was doped," Ringbone

Smith said. "I think there is a shot of poison in it, but they put it in too weak. Instead of killing, it only knocked you out. I doubt if Ed ever got a drink out of it."

"I doubt that, too," Funeral said.

"Pour it down the drain," the printer said.

Funeral uncorked the bottle and poured it down the sink. Old Press got to his feet and stood with his legs wide.

"I'm gettin' my strength back," he said. "That shot the doc gave me is a-helpin' me. He also must have forced something down me, 'cause my mouth has a funny taste."

"Headache tablets, in water," Ringbone said. "You were still groggy but you could swallow."

"I got to get to work," Old Press said "I wonder if I can tell one type from the other?"

"We came over to help," Ringbone said.

"Put on an apron and get to work."

Ringbone got an apron around his

belly and Funeral tied it behind his broad back. Already Old Press was bent over a tray of type.

"I can tell the difference between type-faces," the Negro said, "so I must be gettin' well. Somebody has aimed to poison the boss. By bad luck — or maybe good luck? — I made myself the guinea pig. Somebody aims to kill Ed. I told him he'd get into trouble the minute he filed on that homestead — "

He stopped in the middle of the sentence. Funeral got the impression his befuddled state of mind had made him voice a thought he should not have uttered. And the undertaker was quick to move into the breach.

"Homestead, Old Press?"

The Negro did not look at the mortician. He seemed vitally interested in looking for a certain letter in the pile of type. When he did speak his voice was low and drawling.

"I spoke outa turn, Funeral."

Funeral looked at Ringbone Smith. The veterinarian's mouth was opened slightly

BR11

and his peppermint was not being chewed, now. Ringbone was watching the printer with careful eyes.

"Hand me them pliers over there on that bench?"

Old Press reached a huge hand toward Funeral O'Neill. "Got to lock this type into this case. Done lost my keys somewhere, so I uses them pliers."

Funeral handed him the old pair of pliers. "What was that you said about a homestead, Old Press?"

He watched the Negro closely.

Old Press Johnson shook his head slowly. "I done made a mistake with my tongue. When I said *Homestead* I mean Fred Gittler's homestead. Man, this type case works harder every day."

Funeral said, "You sure you meant Gittler?"

"Forget it, friend, forget it. A slip of the tongue, nothing more. There, I got this frame locked, ready for the press."

Funeral shrugged, then went over to Ed Burnett's desk. He started riffling through the correspondence on the hook and in the drawers. Old Press glanced at him but said nothing; he was working at the flatbed press. Finally Ringbone Smith said, "Ain't a man's correspondence a private thing to you, Funeral?"

"No."

"Well, it should be."

"I never had no upbringing," Funeral O'Neill explained with a wry smile. "I was allowed to shift for myself at the age of six months. When I was a year old I was selling newspapers in the slums of Chicago."

"Hogwash," Ringbone snorted.

Within about ten minutes, the farmer Gittler came in the front door, stomped across the composing room, muddy shoes leaving tracks of water and mud. He sat down in the chair and looked around and said, "I'd sure like to know what happened to me out in that alley. If it was a man that knocked him cold, I'd sure cotton to lay my hands around his neck."

"I don't blame you," Funeral said.

Gittler got to his feet. He roamed

around and he finally took some proof sheets off the hook and read the news for the next edition. He seemed restless and he finally left without saying a word in parting.

Funeral looked at Old Press. "I take it this Gittler fellow and Ed Burnett are good friends, huh?"

"On what grounds do you base that?"

"Well, he came in here just now, read all the proofs, rummaged around, and then left — he seemed to know the place well. He knew where to look for whatever he wanted to read, appeared to me like."

"They know each other," the printer explained, "but I don't think a man could call them close friends — just acquaintances, I'd say."

"Oh, I see."

"You sure are full of questions, Funeral."

"Before I was born my mother was scared by a question mark."

"Right tough luck," the Negro said, and grinned.

Funeral read some proof. Ed Burnett

was right: Old Press could not spell. Finally, after a few minutes, they had another case locked in the old hand press, and Ringbone Smith was given the dubious honor of hand-working the press. He got it rolling and newspapers, printed on one side, went out of the other end.

The ancient hand-press made an awful racket. It was not new. The bearings were poured babbitt, and they had worn down; the rollers jumped and chattered, but it did a fair job of printing, if the ink were heavy enough on the rollers. Ringbone Smith pushed and puffed on the handle. "They makes a motor now to run a press," Old Press hollered above the clatter.

"We need one," Ringbone hollered back, starting to sweat.

"Steam engine," the Negro yelled. "Fire it by wood."

Ringbone Smith looked around for Funeral O'Neill but he had left by the back door. "Where did Funeral go?"

"Heck, I never even heard him leave."

"He didn't want to be caught around here so he'd have to take his turn on this press,'" the veterinary hollered. "He hates all kind of physical labor."

"He sure pulled stakes quiet like."

Funeral, at this moment, was standing in front of the doctor's office, the built-out wooden awning keeping the rain from him. Boxelder was almost completely dark now, except for the saloon, the printing office, the doctor's office, and the jail. He could not see into the office for the blinds had been pulled low. Only a dim crack of light, showing along the base of one blind, told him the lamp was lighted on the inside. He grinned and entered without knocking.

"Howdy, Doc. Oh, shucks, never knew you had a customer, or I wouldn't have barged in on you this way.

The medico had a patient lying on the high table.

He had just finished patching a cut on the man's head. He had shaved the head and the wound was covered with a white patch.

"You sure have no manners, O'Neill," the doctor said.

"Just thought I'd look in and say goodnight," the undertaker returned, apparently paying no attention to the medico's gruffness. He looked at the man on the table who now sat up. "We have had that habit for years, Mr. Henderson. What happened to you, sir?"

Michael Henderson cursed. "None of your damn business," he snarled.

Funeral O'Neill assumed a hurt air. "That isn't a nice way to talk to a man who is interested in your welfare, Mr. Henderson."

"You had no call to bust in here like you did," the doctor said sternly. "This is a private office – a point from where I practice medicine – "

"You forget one thing," the undertaker said.

The doctor studied him belligerently. His bottom lip was twitching. But Funeral knew all the symptoms; he had long known this man of medicine. The doctor was not angry. His lip twitched because he wanted another snort of hard liquor.

"What have I forgot, O'Neill?"

"I am a reporter now – a man of the press. This gives me license to ask questions. The future of this country depends upon a free and unbiased press." He turned his attention to Michael Henderson. "I asked you that question merely from the angle of a reporter seeking a bit of information for his sheet. You do not have to answer, but I did expect a civil reply."

Henderson said, "I'm sorry, O'Neill. I fell down."

"Where at?"

The man hesitated, then said, "In my hotel room. I was just coming in. I tripped over something and my head hit the bureau." He grinned then and added, "If that is news, be free to print it."

"Every incident in this town or on this range is fodder for the Tribune." Funeral had difficulty to keep his mirth from showing. He asked a few other questions. Henderson had Room 14 at the hotel. He seemed somewhat meager as to details of his accident. No, he had not been drinking. Did he have fainting spells? He grew angry again and bristled like a mastiff. "Never fainted in my life," said the fat man soundly and somewhat angrily. "Are you through with your questions, sir?"

"One more, and then that's all."

"What is that?"

"When I write this article, I'll have to state your reason for being in Boxelder, I reckon."

"Why?"

"To make the news complete."

"Just say I'm a visitor in your fair town."

Funeral glanced at him. "All right," he said slowly. "Just a visitor."

The doctor had his bottle uncorked. He raised it and looked over the neck at the mortician.

"An undertaker – a body snatcher – working as a reporter." He raised the bottle and whiskey gurgled in wild abandon down his leather throat. The bottle came down and he said, "Ah . . ." Then his eyes again sought the undertaker. "Seeing you're a reporter, you have to know how to spell, so spell the word *moccasin?*"

Funeral grinned boyishly. "The word had two z's," he said, and left. He went out into the rain, and his smile died. He moved to the end of the street, crossed it, and was opposite the doctor's office, hiding in the darkness of the blacksmith shop's doorway, when the man called Henderson came out of the medico's quarters. Henderson plodded wearily toward the hotel, went into the lobby, and then climbed the stairs to his room.

"Don't stumble again," Funeral said, and smiled.

Then he turned his steps toward the courthouse. There was a light in the office of County Attorney George Parnell and he again entered without knocking Parnell had tons of books on the walls, their bindings dull and lifeless in the lamplight, and he sat in his swivel chair, boots on his desk. His head was down on his huge chest and his lips rumbled as he snored.

Funeral crossed the room and shook him by the shoulder. Parnell opened both eyes and looked up and said sourly, "My God, what a sight. Let me go back to sleep, O'Neill. I'm not dead yet, so hide your needle."

"Wake up, *shyster.*"

The word *shyster* jerked Parnell awake, as Funeral had known it would. He hated the word.

His boots hit the floor.

"O'Neill, that is a fighting word," the lawyer said. Funeral sat down on the bench and grinned. "I knew that would wake you up, George." He looked at the whiskey glass and bottle on the desk. "Since when did you take up Doc's bad habits?"

"Just a bracer, on a cold and windy and rainy night."

Funeral said, "Bad habit. A lone-wolf is the toughest type of imbiber. George, you can help me, fellow."

“What way, gloomy man?”

“We got a newspaper to publish. They call it the Boxelder Tribune. The editor is in your calaboose. We need him because the deadline is tomorrow morning.”

George Parnell shook his head slowly and feigned great boredom. “No can do, even for a body snatcher. Mr. *Edward* – or is it *Edwin* – well, it makes no difference – Mr. Ed Burnett is in jail and the charge is murder. An ugly six lettered word, murder. He cannot be freed on bail until a coroner’s jury either indicts him or frees him. If the indictment is not for first degree murder, he can be released on bail, but if it calls for murder in the first degree, we cannot, under the law, allow him bail. Now is that clear?”

“As muddy water.”

“Having settled that, my friend, would you crave to wet your tonsils with some mountain dew, fresh from the stills south in the Bearpaws. Old Will Wilson used to brew in old Kentucky, but he took his art to Montana, sir, for our pleasure.”

"Maybe for your pleasure," Funeral said sourly, "but not for mine."

"You are a man of few and blunt words. Thank you kindly, sir, for turning down my offer, for it leaves more for my pleasure."

"A friend is a man who helps another in need," Funeral somewhat subtly reminded.

Parnell's eyes were hidden for a moment under drooping lids. "There seems to more than a newspaper editorial involved in this, Funeral. Or do you judge me wrong?"

"I don't know. So . . . I can't judge correctly."

Parnell cupped his hands. He seemed vitally interested in his fingers. "We are indeed friends, Funeral. Fast and good friends . . . I hope. But if you – my friend – got in jail, I would do nothing to release you until the due processes of the Law have ground out their proper verdict."

"Righteous man," Funeral murmured.

He had sarcasm in his voice. This

brought up the heavy head of County Attorney George Parnell. The thick lips moved.

"Bribing an officer of the law, or attempting a bribe, is a felony in this territory, my good man."

Funeral grinned. "Take it easy, you fat jackass. I suppose the jail is open at this hour of the night?"

"Open all night, sir."

"Keep on drinking your young life away."

"With pleasure, sir."

Funeral went down the hall and came to the back door and crossed the yard to the sheriffs office and jail. A lantern, hung on a pole in the middle of the yard, cast out dull rays of light, a big tin reflector turning the rain and keeping it from breaking the chimney. The sheriffs office was empty. Rifles hung from gun racks an the wall and two pistols, still in holsters, hung from hooks on the wall, the dull lamplight reflecting from the cartridges in the loops of the belts. The place was an unguarded arsenal, Funeral figured. If a prisoner broke jail – got into this office with its artillery – He could hold off a small army.

He opened the door leading to the cell block. Here more kerosene lamps held away, pushing back the darkness. Here a man could hear also the rain on the roof much louder for this roof was evidently made of galvanized iron. The rain sounded like hen eggs being dropped on the roof. Funeral walked down the aisle to the cell holding young Ed Burnett. The deputy was still in the cell and they were still playing cards. But Millie Wetherford was not here, now.

Ed Burnett looked up and lamplight showed his strained young-old face. "How is the sheet coming along?" he asked.

"Okay."

"Will it be out before the deadline?"

"I think so."

"Never have run over a deadline yet," Ed said. "I sent some copy down to Old Press. Jailer brought it down there. About an hour or so ago, I guess. Did you get it, Funeral?"

"Being set into type right now."

"Any sheets being run off?"

"Two center pages," the undertaker said. "We could, of course, use your help. You beating the deputy?"

Ed Burnett got to his feet. He walked back and forth. Lamplight played with his shadow, making it first long and then short. His legs were scissors against the far wall, moving like shears as he walked. Dejection pulled at his face, changing it from a boyish face to that of a middle-aged man. He put his hands in his pockets. He looked up and a sharpness was in his eyes.

"Funeral, I got to get out of here. I can't just sit here . . . and play cards, man. I got work to do. And plenty of it."

Funeral shrugged. "Tomorrow, after the coroner's inquest, you'll be free, Ed. They can't hold you for murder."

"You mean that . . . or are you just talking to boost my morale?"

Funeral was doing the latter, but he would be the last to admit this fact.

"For all of me," he said, "I can't see any evidence that can hold you for murder, Ed."

"What if the farmers don't get on the jury. The cowpunchers don't like me. They like Clint Gardner. If the jury gets four cowpunchers, I'm on a murder charge. What about that, Funeral?"

"The jury will be composed of three farmers and three cowpunchers," Funeral O'Neill promised. "I'll see to that. I'm sitting as the head of the inquest, and don't forget that."

"Here comes somebody," Ed Burnett said.

Boots had crossed the office floor. They saw the door open and the deputy had moved forward, hand on his gun. His face was grim. Evidently he was taking this job seriously. And well he had reason, Funeral figured. But tension ran out of the deputy and his hand left his gun.

"Gardner," he said. "Clint Gardner."

Ed Burnett said, "My bosom friend."

Funeral said nothing. Gardner came

down the aisle, boot heels rough on the cement, the echoes running to the darkened corners, and rebounding.

His hat shaded half his face and his features were therefore hard to read. He said, "Howdy, men," and then he stopped, looking at Ed Burnett, there on the other side of the bars. And Funeral saw a cynical smile tear at the man's lips.

"Comfortable, Burnett?" he taunted.

"I'll feel even more comfortable when I have a gun and look at you over the sights," the editor said, his voice a savage whisper.

"That ain't no way to talk to a friend of yours." Gardner was smiling, but with his lips only. His eyes were displeased narrowed slits in his cunning face. "Just checked to see if you were comfortable," he explained.

"Sure nice of you," Ed Burnett said.

The deputy had a face made of hardwood. He chewed his tobacco with slow and frozen deliberation and his eyes moved from one man to the other in cold appraisal. But he said nothing. He just chewed his Horseshoe slowly, molars rising and falling.

Gardner spoke now to Funeral O'Neill. "You're up late, undertaker. For a man of your age, you have nightowl habits."

"You're as old, if not older, than I am," Funeral pointed out carefully, watching the cowman closely.

"This night air is bad for a man." Gardner coughed almost silently, the coughing forced. "I think we all should go home."

Funeral said, "There's the door you came in, Gardner. Nobody has locked it since you came in here."

Gardner held back his anger, but still it added a hard rim to his words. "Somebody should tell you who butters your bread, Undertaker."

"And what do you mean by that?"

The deputy kept on chewing. Ed Burnett watched, hands on the bars. His knuckles were white, his fingers stern on the steel.

"For years the cowman ran this

country," Gardner pointed out with slow deliberation.

"You made a good living then, too, Funeral. Cowmen built this town out of a wilderness spot. These hoemen are adding nothing to it that I can see."

"Maybe your eyes are bad," Funeral said significantly.

"Not that bad," Gardner corrected, shaking his head. "I believe I'll have to warn you, O'Neill."

"On what point?"

"Stick to your own business, undertaker, and stay out of Gardner's way. Is that clear, body-snatcher?"

Funeral grinned. Gardner was seething, and it showed in his lips — this glistened in his eyes, made his hands knotted fists.

"I'll have you on my slab . . . yet," Funeral said."You might be there ahead of me." Gardner turned, took a step, then turned back, eyes gimlet sharp. "Did you get that check I wrote you?"

"I did. But one thing surprised me."

"And that?"

"Never knew before you could write."

Gardner did not rise for the bait. He spoke with sardonic softness now, his temper having run its wild course.

"I can write, and I can handle a gun, too."

"And I can do the same," cut in Ed Burnett.

Gardner sent a glance at the publisher, and then went down the aisle toward the door. His boots were even harder on the cement, now. He shut the door with a wicked sound, and this ran through the jail and then died, and the rain was heard again – pelting and landing and dripping.

Funeral had to make his play soon, and now was as good a time as any time. He peered at the single high window.

"Somebody just looked in there," he said excitedly.

The deputy turned toward the window, and Ed Burnett followed suit. The deputy walked the length of the cell toward the window, head up as he watched the aperture. Funeral dug the .45 out of his belt and pushed it against Ed Burnett's back. Ed turned and saw the Colt pistol and grabbed it and with one sharp gesture pushed it under the blanket on the bed. This took no time at all. Ed's eyes thanked Funeral. His lips moved, but no words came. The deputy turned, looked at Funeral, and he said, "I saw nobody at the window."

"I'm danged sure," Funeral said.

Harshness ran across the deputy's homely face, giving his words a savage color. "I've stood enough for one night, Funeral. Visiting hours are over, man. Lock that front door as you go out. We've had enough company for one night."

Funeral shrugged, said, "I still maintain somebody looked in that window. Well, just as you say, lawman."

"Time to move, Funeral."

Funeral O'Neill smiled. "Don't be so rough on the county coroner. I don't want to go out the front door. I want to go out the back door."

"Why?"

"I'm going home, and the alley is the closest route."

"The back door is locked."

"You can unlock it."

The deputy grumbled, "Oh, go out the front," and then he reconsidered. After all, Funeral did hold down a county job — an important job, too. And a man had to play politics.

"You're a damned nuisance, but I guess I got to oblige."

The deputy unlocked the cell door and locked it again. Funeral wanted to get the deputy out of the cell so Ed Burnett could get the gun out from under the blanket. He had never before helped in a jail delivery. To put it midly, he was rather nervous; he hoped this would work. If it did not work — if the deputy went for his gun — He wished he had not smuggled the .45 to Ed Burnett. But he had done it. He wondered if Ed would recognize his own gun. He had taken the gun from the desk in the Tribune office.

Maybe he had done wrong? He had a

hundred conflicts in him. They came to the door. It was bolted and the deputy unbolted it. At this moment Funeral glanced back at Ed Burnett, who waved to him. Burnett packed a wide smile. A smile so wide he could see it clearly despite the uncertain light.

"So long," the deputy said.

Funeral O'Neill stepped into the alley. He got a sudden shock. The rain had stopped. The clouds had fallen back, split by a high hard wind, and the moon was actually shining. Moonlight washed across Boxelder, showing chimneys and houses, glistening on windows. Had the rain stopped for good?

He hoped so. He, for one, had had enough rain.

But his mind did not dwell long on the rain or the weather. He had more important things to think about. He went down the alley, picking his way through the mud. The deputy would be in for a rough evening. Not too rough, he hoped: He suddenly moved back into the protection of a shadow, his back against a shed. He had his .45 in his hand and he hardly remembered pulling the gun.

A man was coming toward him.

He was big and wide and huge in the moonlight.

He ambled forward slowly. Funeral thought, I'd know that man anywhere, just by his outline, and he holstered his gun. He moved forward and the man, for the first time, saw him. The man stopped, then came ahead again; they met.

"Howdy, O'Neill," the man said. He had a deep voice that rumbled in his chest, a gruff and heavy voice.

"Mr. Henderson,'" Funeral said.

They looked at each other and were silent for a moment. Funeral got the impression that this man was feeling him out. There was this curtain between them, and it sparkled and twisted, charged there in the moonlight. Funeral O'Neill was acutely aware of this; he was sure that Michael Henderson was, also.

Funeral said, "You have a bad habit, Mr. Henderson."

"And that habit, sir?"

"You walk down alleys all the time . . . instead of using the main street. This is the second time tonight you have been meandering down an alley in this town."

"I could say the same about you, too."

Funeral said, "But I'm heading for my bunk."

"So am I. Heading for my hotel room."

Funeral nodded, and held his tongue for a long moment. Across town a bevy of curs took up a savage loud barking. The noise ran across the roofs, hit the chimneys, and became lost in the wind.

He did not remind the obese man that he was going out of his way to get to his hotel. There was no use in offering this information for he felt sure that Michael Henderson would find nothing new or startling in this disclosure.

"We walk together then for a ways," the undertaker said.

They walked about a block together.. They came to the back stairway of the hotel. Here they parted.

Henderson said, "This back door is locked. I have to go in the front. Good night, sir, and good dreams."

"The same to you, sir."

Henderson halted, looked at the moon. For a moment his face was very clear. The thick lips stood out, the nose was broad and big, the eyes were steer big under the heavy lids.

"A nice night."

"Hope the rain stays away for a while."

"Good for the farmers."

"They've had enough."

Henderson moved then, going between the two buildings. His bulk filled the opening. He was out of sight. Funeral had a cold feeling along his back for some odd reason. This cold area moved, and danced, and then left. His own office was about four houses down the alley. He went in by the back door.

This way he would have to walk around the slab holding Colt Hagen and old man Quinn. The air was close in the closed room. There was in it the smell of death — dry and acrid and dusty death. But Funeral O'Neill had long ago inured his nostrils to such a smell. It had become commonplace, an everyday odor.

He stood there for a moment, then he moved around the slab, and went to the front part of the building, where he had his living quarters. He went out the front door, silently shutting it behind him.

He moved along the building's side, the logs rough against his hands. He stopped and looked into the alley. He was hidden there and he crouched and watched, his .45 in his hand.

He saw nothing, heard nothing of danger. The dogs barked again, loud and savage; they were clicking their fangs. Beyond town a coyote howled and the loneliness of his yelping sang across the moonlight. This brought the dogs to greater talking, and their speech was loud and insistent. Idly the undertaker noticed that the source of the barking, the spot whereon the canines stood, remained stationary. At this he smiled absently. The dogs were not moving away from their homestead. Had they ran out into the brush, the coyotes would have circled them and dined off their flesh. The mutts were wise.

After a while, a man came out of the shadows, there across the street. Openly he moved down the strip. He was wide and huge and he ambled as he walked, hands down low on his sides.

Funeral would know that outline anywhere.

Funeral O'Neill added this all together, seeking the sum total. Michael Henderson had not gone to his hotel. He had trailed him and watched and seen him go into the funeral home.

Then he had remained behind about twenty minutes. He had hidden his bulk in the shadows . . . and he had watched the back door. He had spied on him.

And why?

Funeral O'Neill was never a man to waste too much time in conjecture. He believed that thought — deliberate and deductive thinking – was all right in its place but some times the answer lay in action – hard and fast action. Now was probably one of these times, he reasoned.

He and Ringbone Smith had a barn on the edge of town, far enough out so the odors would not reach the town unless the wind blew hard from that direction. Now he went to this barn. They had four head of saddle-horses in the barn. Two of these horses were also broken to be wagon-horses.

Sometimes Funeral, in slack periods of work, would go out on trips with his partner, who many times was called to far distant ranches, some as far as sixty to seventy miles away. He came into the barn and he talked to the horses; one, though, snorted.

The undertaker did not light a lantern. He did not want to disclose his visit to his barn. He worked in the dark. He talked softly to the horses. He knew where the gear was, and he saddled two of the broncs. It was rather difficult to do in the dark. He wanted to light a lantern, but discretion forbade this.

He worked as fast as he could in the dark. He found saddle blankets and put them on the horses, straightening the wrinkle out of them. A wrinkle in a saddle blanket would put a saddle-gall on a horse.

This done to his satisfaction, he lowered down the saddles. He caught the cinch on the one horse's saddle, slipped the tackaberry buckle around the cinch-ring, and pulled the latigo tight, finding the hole for the tongue to go into. Then he saddled the other horse. This saddle had no tackaberry buckle. He laced the latigo strap through the ring and made his tie and put the loose end up in the latigo-holder. Then he bridled both horses. He left the hackamores on them. He led them out the back door and down the alley and came to the rear door of the printing shop. He hammered on this and Ringbone Smith, still wearing the dirty leather apron, let him in. Ringbone did not see the horses out there in the alley.

"What is the matter with you, Funeral?" the vet asked.

"Nothing," the undertaker said, pretending he did not understand. "What do you mean, partner?"

The veterinarian snorted. He had an ink splotch on the side of his nose. "You know full well what I mean, O'Neill! You been dartin' hither and yon like a hen with her head cut off! We got a newspaper to set and run off, and we need your help – yet you bat around like a loco yearling."

Old Press was rummaging through a desk. He had evidently already gone through Ed Burnett's desk for the drawers were open. He had the harried look of a man who had seen a certain object a moment before and then, when he had turned around, had not seen it – it had disappeared.

"What's wrong with him?" Funeral asked.

"Ed Burnett's pistol is gone, he claims."

"Well, I'll be dogged," Funeral said.

Old Press Johnson had wide eyes. "Danged funny thing, too. Was right there in that drawer about a hour ago.

I done seen it there. Now it's done gone."

"Maybe somebody has pilfered it," Funeral offered.

The man shook his head sagely. "Nobody in here but me an' Ringbone, Funeral. But the gun is done gone."

"Might have floated off." Funeral grinned.

Old Press scratched his wiry hair. The noise was that of a farmer rubbing off a hog's bristles.

"Got me buffaloed."

"I don't know where it could – "

Funeral O'Neill never got to finish his sentence. That was because from outside down the alley came the stabbing roar of a six-shooter. The blasting concussion broke through the moonlight, smashed across the town of Boxelder, and then ran off into space against the sagebrush covered flats surrounding the cowtown. Unconsciously Funeral counted two shots. Judging by their sounds they had evidently come from two different guns. He judged both as being six-shooters. .45s, probably, judging from the sounds.

Then, the roar was dead. The canines took up a wild and startled barking. Ringbone Smith was poised, mouth open, peppermint suspended between his teeth, a galley in his hands. Funeral glanced at Old Press Johnson. The Negro stood solid, head canted.

"That come from the jail," Old Press said shakily.

The printer started for the back door. Ringbone Smith dropped the galley-tray, the type slipping unnoticed to the stone, and he started after the Negro, who was almost to the door. Funeral O'Neill reached out and snagged his partner by the forearm, stopping him.

Ringbone Smith had round eyes. "Why hold me back? That shootin' sure as hell come from the jail."

"No use going out there, friend."

"No use? O'Neill have you gone plumb loco? That came from the jail – and Ed is in there – if Gardner has murdered him – Let go of me."

Funeral let his hand drop. "Nothing

we could do any way," he said. Fear was in him and he hoped his voice did not betray this. Had Ed and the deputy shot it out? He hoped not. He liked Carl and he liked Ed – Maybe he had done wrong in smuggling the publisher his .45? For a moment he was torn by doubts and anxieties. He was sure of only one thing – if Ed had got himself killed, he, Funeral O'Neill, would carry the scar on his soul until he died. But he doubted if Ed would shoot at Carl. He would slug the deputy and tie him up and get his keys and make his escape that way. He would not shoot it out with Carl. Funeral felt some relief at this thought. His theory was that Ed had walked out the back door and into gunflame –

"I don't follow you, Funeral. Usually you are the first man to run for a fire or a shooting."

"Well, all right, pal."

They stepped out into a night bright with moonlight that was shattered by the howling of dogs and the yelling of people. The town of Boxelder, Territory of Montana, was on the move – gunfire had jerked citizens out of sound sleep and warm beds. They were converging on the jail. Some pulled up pants and others tugged on shirts. Women were out in robes and slippers despite the mud. Only lady Jones, who ran the boarding house, slipped in the mud, skidded on her wide and ample bottom, and showed the world an expanse of thighs, as her nightgown slid upward. Then she was on her way again, not stopping to even brush mud from her robe.

Funeral did not want to get close to the jail. The thought persisted that, if the deputy had killed Ed, then the deputy would raise a big holler, pointing to him, Funeral O'Neill, as the man who had smuggled the .45 into the cell of his prisoner. Temptation was strong in the undertaker to go and see what had happened. This conflicted with the element of personal danger. He remembered how Michael Henderson had watched the back of the jail. Funeral had deliberately pulled him away by inviting him to walk home with him. Had Henderson returned to his post behind the jail and had he shot down Ed Burnett as he had come out of the door after slugging and tying up the deputy?

A boy of about ten, running hard, came toward them, and the undertaker snagged him by the right arm, swinging him around to a sliding halt.

"You been to the jail, Sonny?"

Sonny Webster panted like a young bull on a hot July day. "Ed Burnett done busted out of the calaboose, Mr. O'Neill. He knocked the deputy – Carl Shultz – he knocked Carl cold."

"Who did he fight with – and did he get away?"

Funeral thought, was that my voice? Sounds like a magpie croaking on a fence post, it does.

"He fought with Williams, that Gardner gink. You know him, Funeral. Ed done shot him down."

"Williams," Ringbone Smith repeated.

"What do you reckon he was doing behind that jail, Funeral?"

"Gardner had him there as a guard, I guess. How bad is Williams off, Sonny. Or is he dead?"

The boy did not know for sure. He was hurrying for the doctor. Williams was still alive, though. He had to get on his way. Funeral accordingly released him. Sonny disappeared into the moonlight like an ant darting down a dark hole in the ground.

"Williams done said to Gardner that he was heading for the Circle S," Ringbone Smith said. "Gardner said he was going to stay in the hotel and Williams was going to the ranch – yet here he shows up shootin' at Ed Burnett."

Funeral said nothing. He listened to the babble of voices. He felt as though two tons of weight had been pulled off his shoulder. He knew he would have to stay away from the deputy. The man would claim for sure that he, Funeral O'Neill, had smuggled the gun into Ed's cell. Hard on this thought came the next question from Ringbone Smith.

"Wonder how Ed got hold of a gun?"

Funeral had a sudden plan. "Maybe Millie Wetherford smuggled him his gun," he said. "She might have got it from the office, you know."

"But she couldn't have smuggled him his own gun," the veterinarian pointed out quickly. "She wasn't in the office at the time we missed it"

Another boy came along. They got more information out of him. He was going to see why the first boy had not returned with the doctor. Funeral figured that the medico was probably out cold from drink on his bunk. Ed Burnett had made good his escape. Dunlap was running around in circles. He was getting a posse ready to ride out and look for Ed.

"Wonder where he got a horse?" Ringbone asked the boy.

"Some claim Williams he had a horse back in the alley," the boy said, and hurried on.

Ringbone said, "Well, I'll be plumb

sagged back, but this has me stumped. Williams had no reason to be behind the jail. He said he was gonna head for the Gardner ranch. Don't make no logic to me, does it to you?"

"A little, Ringbone."

"It does! Well, how much?" Ringbone Smith did not await an answer. A suspicious edge rimmed his next words. "Somehow I think you got a hand in this, O'Neill. Seems odd you didn't cotton to running right off up the alley. That has me puzzled. Hey, let go of my arm! Where you takin' me?"

"A night ride is ahead of us, Ringbone."

"A night ride? Mister, have you gone loco. Say, where you going, man? Headin' up the alley this way, grabbin' me by the arm."

"Come along, and shut up."

They came to the point where Funeral had tied the two saddled horses. But there was only one horse there now. He understood. Ed Burnett had not headed out on Williams' horse. He had taken one of the horses Funeral had saddled, just as the undertaker had figured.

"This is my hoss," Ringbone said. "Tied here in the dark. Funeral, you saddled him – you knew this was coming."

"I had another saddled," the funeral-director said, "but Ed must have taken him. Just as I figured."

"Tell me, Funeral?"

"After we get started, man. We'll get Ed's bronc. He's in the barn behind the print shop. Good thing he never tried to get him. Guns might have cut him down. By the time he could have covered the distance from the jail to the barn, the guns would have been booming."

"Where we headin' for?"

Funeral O'Neill neglected to answer this question.

He liked to torment his partner and to accomplish this end he decided to keep him in doubt for some time. Two men hurried by, running for their homes and their horses.

"Ed Burnett done busted out of the jail, men," one called to them. "We're going to build a posse and head out after him. Sheriff Dunlap orders every able-bodied man in Boxelder into saddle, so you had best climb your stirrups."

Then, they were gone, swallowed by the moonlit night.

"I have to get another horse," Funeral O'Neill said, and started for their barn on the run. Once he slipped and almost fell in the mud. He silently cursed the mud. He had had enough mud to last him the rest of his life. He was tired of trouble, too. All this trouble had taken place inside of one day. And that day seemed miles long to him now. It seemed ages ago since Millie Wetherford had shaken him awake there in his office to tell him about the killing of Colt Hagen.

The thought of the posse trailing down young Ed Barnett made him smile grimly. They could never find the young printer in this night. Even with bright moonlight, vision was strictly curtailed; tracks would and could tell nothing, for the rain had made the earth soft and many horses had moved across it, leaving their shod or unshod imprints. And, also, a man cannot trail in the dark, even if he had eyes supposedly as sharp as those of a cat.

Ed had a good headstart. He would make good his escape. But now he had two murder charges against him, for his gun had knocked down Williams. Then the thought came that Williams was not dead. But, if the man died, the score against Ed Burnett would double. Again doubt touched the bony undertaker. Maybe he should have left Ed in jail? But he had been afraid one of Gardner's gunmen – or Gardner himself – might murder the printer. It had been done before; it could have been done again. Gardner was playing marbles for keeps, he knew.

He dashed into the barn and got the smells of saddle-leather, of horseflesh, of musty hay, of strong new manure. He led out a sorrel gelding, carrying a saddle in one hand, the blanket curled over his arm. The blanket went into place and the saddle, lifted in the air, seemed to be suspended for a moment, there against the moon – then it came down with a resounding whack on the horse's back. One sweep, he had the cinch; he made his latigo tie.

By this time, Ringbone Smith had ridden out of the night, and he leaned down and handed his partner a Winchester .30-30 rifle.

"Rode down to my shack," the veterinarian said, "and got my spare rifle. Also picked up some cartridges for it and our short-guns."

"Good work, Ringbone."

Ringbone Smith leaned back, hands on the fork of his saddle, and he stretched in leather, saddle creaking.

"Good to be in a kak," he said. "Be hell to live in a city for good. Stale air, bad eggs, no horse to wrap your legs around. Not for this cow nurse. By the way, O'Neill, take down your hair, man. Unlimber to your Uncle?"

Funeral found his stirrup. His left boot went into it and the sorrel reared, struggling against the severity of the reins. Then the angular body of the undertaker lifted, then settled; his right boot hooked the stirrup. The rifle twisted around in his hands so the barrel was down and it slid into the leather saddle-holster smoothly, whispering against the slick cowhide.

Funeral reined the sorrel around and said, "I don't quite follow you in your line of thought."

"Where – are – we – going?"

"I'll tell you when we get on the trail, Ringbone."

Ringbone Smith spat into the mud. From across town came the baying of dogs, the rattle of men's voices, and suddenly the neigh of a horse cut through these sounds, clear and stern and challenging.

"Don't act so mysterious, O'Neill. I can tell you one thing for sure – for damned sure, fellow."

"And that, Ringbone?"

The veterinarian had a harsh voice. He leaned low over his saddle and his eyes were hollow and stabbing

"I'm not trailing my friend, Ed Burnett. If he downed that Williams dog – if he finally dies – Williams, that is – Well, more power to Ed. Gardner has dogged that young man day and night, night and day. And if Ed kills Gardner, more power to Ed, I say."

Funeral was surprised at the hardness in his partner's voice. Usually Ringbone Smith was an easy-going man but tonight he was made of molten steel.

"We aren't going to try and trail Ed," the undertaker assured.

"Then what are we going to do?"

"We're going to help Ed, of course." Funeral O'Neill neckreined his plunging mount around. "Come on, cow nurse."

"Right with you, body snatcher."

Funeral O'Neill took the lead. They left Boxelder town on a hard smashing lope. Behind the undertaker's horse plunged the bronc carrying Ringbone Smith who rode like a fat monkey, perched on his stirrups, bent over the neck of his mount. Funeral was bent over, too, but he looked like a gaunt question-mark that had suddenly taken life and had found a saddle.

A group of men were coming down mainstreet. They were in the act of crossing the street when the partners slanted around a corner and came roaring down on them. Funeral lifted his voice in loud tones.

"O'Neill and Smith, riding out. Going to catch us a bandit, men. Out of the way, boys."

"Scatter," a man hollered.

They scattered like young sagehens breaking up in front of a coyote. One man, in his haste, slipped on his belly, landing face down in the mud. Funeral glimpsed his mud-stained face, water dripping from his beard, as he rode by, hoofs coming down fast. He recognized the man.

The man cursed him in loud tone, using vile language. Funeral twisted in saddle, laughing for a moment.

"Don't curse me, Wiggins. 'Cause sooner or later, I'll get my embalming needle in you, and I'll get it in deep in a vein."

"You grave-robber!"

Ringbone Smith said, "He's mad. He might use his gun."

"Gun slid out of holster when he went down," Funeral grunted, not caring whether or not his partner heard. "Full of mud and water, that .45 is, and now out of business."

They went around another corner. Funeral's horse slipped, laid on his side, slid about ten feet, then got to his feet, his rider resuming his seat. And then the undertaker was whipping his horse to catch the mount ridden by his partner.

Ringbone Smith was still hunched over his horn, slicker spread out behind him. He had a sack tied across the back of his saddle and it bounced with each jolting jump of his horse. Funeral guessed this carried ammunition – shells for their .45s and their Winchesters. With difficulty his horse crept even with that of Ringbone's. They were out on the prairie racing south. Funeral gave his surroundings a casual glance, instantly reckoning their position on this wilderness expanse. They were following the wagon-trail that led to the farmers' settlement. This twisted through the gray wet sagebrush, darker than the brush and looking like a wide black ribbon, uncoiling through the waist-high sagebrush.

The rain had freshed the sagebrush, bringing it into strong odor. This odor washed across the plains, pleasant in its strength. A jackrabbit, scared out of his hiding place, leaped out of the brush and hit the trail, running ahead of them. He ran with reckless abandon, ears back and his long hind legs reaching up so far they kicked his ears and then, his pleasure supplied, he zigzagged off the trail, darted into the brush, and was seen no longer.

Ringbone looked at him. The wind had pushed back his old hat and he looked somewhat like an old Indian scout, Funeral thought absently.

Now, Mister Undertaker, talk to

your partner.

Funeral O'Neill leaned toward his partner, nigh boot anchored in stirrups to hold his weight. He had to holler but he explained in just a few words. Moonlight showed first puzzlement, then utter surprise, and then these became supplanted by a look that spoke of stern anger.

"The dirty dogs," the veterinarian snarled.

Funeral straightened, getting his seat firmly. A satanic grin was on his death-head of a face. His lips were close and bloodless, his eyes sunken and roving, and his high cheekbones stood up and were clear in the parchment-like skin. But he said nothing, having only his thoughts for companions.

"Only a hunch, though," he yelled, "and nothing more. Nothing of concrete nature, my friend, only a strong hunch."

"Backed up some evidence, though," the veterinarian hollered back. "A dirty plot, sired by greed — a man is a hungry thing."

"For dollars, yes. For affection and love — the worthwhile things in life — I have to say no. He does not merit love, in most cases."

"Always an exception to every case, and don't forget that."

"I'm thinking now of Millie Wetherford," the undertaker said.

Ringbone Smith said, "And a fine woman she is, too. She'll make a wonderful wife, and her children will be fine lads and lassies. Her home will be well managed, and her husband and children will be proud of her."

Funeral said, "Never knew you could get so poetic. Why is it that a man of such sterling thought never himself got hitched double?"

"Never had any time to contemplate matrimony with any deep seriousness."

Funeral had a face that was as dead as a sheep hide. "You stated that wrong," he said. "You should amend it."

"To what degree?"

"The superlative. No woman, my friend, would have you."

Funeral heard his partner's scoffing laugh. "How about Nellie?"

"She didn't marry you, remember. She took on Bill Overstreet, leaving you in the ditch."

A low laugh. "She married Bill . . . because I wouldn't hook up with her." Ringbone Smith pulled down his mount to a slower lope. Now seriousness possessed him and drove away the last traces of frivolity. "Let's quit the joking, Funeral. This is no joking matter."

"Reckon you're right there, friend."

"Where do we head for first, Funeral?"

Funeral O'Neill had a serious face now. Gone was the laughter and the smile. In its place was studied seriousness. The thin lips of the undertaker moved slowly but his words were clear, for they were walking their broncs now and the wet soil muffled their hoofbeats.

"Clint Gardner," he said.

"What about him?"

"Look at it from Gardner's viewpoint. Gardner cannot afford to let Ed Burnett live. Gardner has to kill Burnett. But first, we head for Fred Gittler's homestead, and we check there."

"Good idea."

"We might be . . . too late."

"Got to take that chance, Funeral."

"Let's drift."

When they rode into the yard of the Gittler homestead the sod shack was dark. The sod shack was where the hired man slept, Ringbone said. But beyond the sod house, at the foot of Rising Butte, was the main house, and it had no light either. Back of the spread towered the igneous lift of Rising Butte, coming out of the plains to rear its rocky crust upward. The shadow of it was across the land, engulfing the homestead buildings.

They loped in, horses breathing heavily, and when they went past the sod shack Funeral O'Neill hollered, "Two riders coming in. Funeral O'Neill and Ringbone Smith, of Boxelder."

Then it was that two dogs, aroused from their slumber in the sod shack, came running out the door, snapping and growling. They were fierce mongrels, trained to kill coyotes, and one came snarling in, intending to gnaw the hamstrings of the undertaker's bronc's hind leg. The horse kicked and the bronc's hoof was sure. His shod hoof hit the cur in the shoulder, the caulks ripping his hide and knocking him sprawling. He scrambled to his feet and fled back into the shack, yipping in pain and terror. His partner, surprised at the harsh reception given his canine associate, kept his distance, but his barks were loud and insistent in their savage cadence.

"They must be using the sod shack for a dog house," the undertaker hollered.

"No money to hire a hired man, I reckon. Well, here we are – at the main house – nice building – Gittler must have brought some money in." Ringbone Smith curbed his horse. He hollered, "Mrs. Gittler, two friendly riders."

For a moment, there was a silence, broken only by the heaving ribs of their horses making saddle-leather creak, by the horses gasping for air. The dog was done, his barking through.

From the saturated soil came the smell of water. Somewhere a flower bloomed, and the aroma was on the air. Its sweetness did not fit into the harshness of Funeral O'Neill's thoughts.

"Gittler," called the undertaker.

Now the door of the house opened. They saw the form come out, and both knew it was a woman. She carried a rifle. Moonlight showed on the barrel for the rifle was old and the bluing had worn thin, the metal shiny.

"I'm Mrs. Gittler," a low voice said.

Down came their hats. And it was the low voice of Funeral O'Neill that took over. "We're sob to barge in at this hour of the night,madam, and we apologize for our rudeness. But we have to see your husband."

"My husband is not home."

Was there something in her voice? Funeral gave this brief thought. Was it fear, or relief?

"He didn't come home from town yet," she said.

He had now pegged the something as being emotion, for her voice was not steady, and a naked fear seemed to underlie her words. Now her voice rose and became a squeaky fear.

"My husband – he has left town – or you two wouldn't be out here looking for him. You wouldn't think he was at home. Has something happened to – Fred?" She leaned the rifle against the wall and came forward and peered up at them. She was a small woman, not over five feet tall, and she had a robe wrapped around her small body, tight and firm. Moonlight showed her eyes, and they were wild with fear. They were as wild as her voice.

"Did Fred – leave town – for his home?"

Funeral O'Neill nodded. "Mr. Gittler left town some time ago," he said.

"And they – " She stopped. "And he should have been home . . . by now?"

"By all rights, madam, yes," the mortician soothed.

She caught herself and stiffened. You

could almost feel the tension go into her small body.

"They have killed him. Murdered him. They're ruthless. They will kill to get what they want. Oh, how I wish – "

She did not finish the sentence. She turned and went into the house, picking up the rifle. The door went shut softly and easily behind her. From the interior of the house came the sudden wail of small children. This cut through both of the partners with the sharpeness of a razor blade. They turned their horses. They rode slowly away. They rode slowly because they did not want to make any noise. Noise would disturb this family that was bound in its own rigid sorrow.

The dogs did not bark. They lay in the dark shadow of the sod house and they bristled and growled but did not bark or run out. When they got beyond the sight of the house, they drew reins. And Ringbone Smith, bearlike in his saddle, leaned forward, viewing his partner with a studied glance.

"So far, Funeral, your guess work has been okay."

Funeral O'Neill stood on his stirrups and looked at high Rising Butte, and its dark shadow cast across the wet and steaming earth. But the shadow, black as it was, did not cover all the igneous dike of rock, there at the base of the butte. This ledge lifted itself a few feet from the earth, a black streak of once molted rock, a streak smearing the earth, marking it with blackness. Then it pitched and ran out, losing itself within a distance of about half a mile.

The right hand of Funeral O'Neill, a gaunt claw in the moonlight, lifted and pointed to the beginning and end of this ledge.

"That ledge is almost all on Gittler's land, as you can see. Yonder it runs off and peters out, but his confines hold it almost in its entirety. What do you say, friend? Where is Fred Gittler?"

"That speaks for itself, I think."

"He left Boxelder . . . but he never reached home."

"I feel it in my bones," Ringbone said, and almost shuddered. "I think his body is somewhere in this sagebrush ahead."

"But we rode out the road from town, and saw no horse or body on it."

"We didn't come the short cut."

Funeral looked to the northwest. "He might have taken the short cut, at that. Though the badland trail would be hard to ride this time of the night, what with mud making it slippery and those canyon deep."

"We got to ride that way."

Ringbone said, "I'm thinking of that little woman and those wailing children. And we might have another mark against Clint Gardner."

"Maybe."

Ringbone Smith said, "Come on," and then he added, "We talk as though he is dead. He might not be."

They loped toward the badlands, barely discernible ahead. They looked low and ominous, dark against the moonlight. They rode at a slow lope. They figured their mounts would have many miles ahead of them before morning; there was no percentage in killing off horseflesh. Funeral leaned and his eyes sparkled in the moonlight. His words were muffled by the hoofbeats.

"Like she said, they're ruthless. There's a fortune at stake. They want it. They'll kill to get it. The strings are running shut."

"And fast," Ringbone Smith said.

Funeral O'Neill straightened. "I had to turn Ed loose. They would have killed him and that deputy, both, to get to Ed. Williams must have taken Henderson's place, when I pulled him away from the jail."

"That is water under the bridge, Funeral."

"It all goes down to this," Funeral O'Neill said. "A dead man cannot sign a legal document."

"Reckon that is it, Shylock."

"He might have fled for his life," the undertaker said, "because surely he must know the odds against him. He might have headed back into the hills with his rifle and he might intend to sneak down and notify his wife later."

"Let's hope so."

But the veterinarian's voice held a pessimistic note that Funeral O'Neill could not overlook. They were entering the badlands, which were about three miles from the Gittler farm. A man could cross the rough country with a saddlehorse but there was no wagon trail through this country of odd-shaped buttes, of many colors and rough couless. They did not have to ride into the badlands. For, where the trail left the rough region, they saw a horse ahead — a horse that bore a saddle. And Funeral O'Neill, riding in the lead, hollered back, "A bronc ahead, Ringbone."

"Looks like Gittler's gray horse to me," the vet hollered back.

And so it turned out to be. The gray, a big horse with collar sores, stood to one side; reins on the ground. His reins, Funeral noticed quickly, were tied together; the mark of an unexperienced saddleman. A cowpuncher never tied his reins together. This was for the simple reason that if he got thrown from his horse the reins would fall and hit the ground and the saddle-horse, trained to stop when his reins trailed, could not run off and leave the man alone. But this horse had evidently run away from the scene of the ambushing, and, stopping to graze, had allowed his reins to slip down his mane, go over his head, and then ground-tie him.

Funeral dismounted, walked up to the gray. The horse was spooky. He tried to get away. Funeral grabbed the reins and held him. He reached up and touched the fork of the saddle and his hand came down sticky and covered with a heavy fluid. He touched his tongue to his hand.

"Blood," he told Ringbone.

"Ambush."

Funeral went back to his horse and remounted. He looked at the trail leading into the badlands.

"Somewhere back there," he said.

Ringbone Smith nodded. He dug for

a peppermint. "How old was the blood?" He jammed the peppermint between his teeth.

"About an hour old, I'd say. And I should know because of my profession." The undertaker had a grim smile.

"Looks this way to me," Ringbone said, speaking around the peppermint. "They've dumped him from his saddle. But because of them tied reins his horse got away. By all rights they would kill the horse, too. Then bury both horse and rider. But the bronc got away."

"So it would appear to me, too."

"Well, let's hope we don't ride into an ambush, too.

"Come along," the undertaker said, and took the lead. They did not ride into any ambush. The trail was one of danger. They rode along edges wide enough to accomodate only a single horse. Then sometimes the trail would widen, but not much. This was ideal country for an ambush. The weirdness of the land, the eeriness of it, struck a chord in the undertaker, giving him a coldness not brought on by the night chill. He was glad when they found the dead man. Gittler lay in the brush on the side of the trail. They would never have found him had not their horses shied at the smell of newly-fresh blood. They shyed suddenly, curling under their saddles, and then the pair quieted their mounts, got out of saddles and went into the underbrush. And it was Funeral O'Neill who almost stumbled over the dead man.

"Here, Ringbone; over here."

By the time the puffing Ringbone Smith arrived, Funeral O'Neill had already got to his feet after testing the man's heartbeat.

"Dead," he said. "Bullet through his chest and head."

"His wife a widow, his children without a father," Ringbone Smith said tonelessly. "Wonder if Clint Gardner ambushed him, or did he send out one of his gunhands?"

"Remains to be found out."

Ringbone walked away and stood in

thought. Funeral moved over and stood beside his partner. Here the night was quiet. Because of the butte behind them there was no wind. No nightbirds broke the silence. The moonlight was silent, the land was silent, and both felt and appreciated these moods. Funeral did not know all the details, the corners, of this thing. But he knew some things, for certain. There was a fortune at stake. Those letters he had read – those letters hidden under the hotel's mattress – they had told him much. Also he had found some data in young Ed Burnett's desk. This had helped tie together the strong strings. Then Old Press Johnson had let slip about the *homestead* – Ed Burnett's homestead. All these things now moved together in the undertaker's mind, seeking a compact wholeness. But the whole thing was not clear, the strings had not been woven in solidly, and there was something ahead, and only Time would disclose that.

These elements, when compounded together, when added one to the other, spelled but one word, and that word was D A N G E R ! And that meant, to young Ed Burnett, only one thing, and that word was D A N G E R! Funeral wondered where the youth was. Ed Burnett had drifted out, and he had made good his escape. These were things in his favor, the undertaker realized.

"What do we do now?" Ringbone Smith asked.

For a moment a sort of futile anger gripped the undertaker. And it showed in his voice as he said, "Who directed your thoughts and took care of you before we met, Ringbone?"

"Don't get snorty with me, or I'll be forced to trim you down."

Funeral O'Neill smiled then, anger momentarily forgotten. "Sorry, old timer," he murmured. "But sometimes things pile up fast and heavy."

"Never too heavy or too fast to save a young man's life. Especially when the young man has as much promise as has Ed Burnett, and with a girl like Millie waiting for him."

Funeral glanced at his partner. "Well said," he replied.

"What is next, then?"

Funeral O'Neill answered with slow heaviness. "I believe we have kin of overlooked one thing, friend."

"And that?"

"Maybe Gittler killed the man who ambushed him?"

Ringbone Smith rolled a peppermint. He got it upright between his molars crushed it with a noise of finality.

"You are right."

"We search then for a few minutes," Funeral said. "You take the south, and I take the north. Not more than a quarter mile each way from this point, though. That okay?"

"Good."

This time it was Ringbone Smith, the veterinarian, who found the evidence. First he found a horse tied to a bunch of brush, hidden by the underbrush. The horse was a black gelding. He bore the Gardner brand. Then he found the dead man. He had evidently been shot in the ruckus and had tried to get to his hidden horse. But he had not made it.

He called his partner over. Then he waited. He could hear Funeral crackling his way through the brush. He called again so the undertaker could place the spot where he stood.

"Dead man, Funeral."

Funeral O'Neill stood on wide-spread legs and panted. Ringbone had rolled the man over on his back. Now he went down again and lit a match and for a moment the yellow flare played across the gaunt dead face with its lackluster eyes, its mouth open. Then, the match died.

"Bert Stanley," Funeral O'Neill said. "A Gardner gunman."

Funeral nodded. "Sent out to ambush and kill Gittler. But Gittler plugged him, in the process. We never did find Gittler's rifle."

"Must have become lost in the brush."

"Makes no never-mind."

Ringbone wiped his hands on his slicker. He wiped them palm down and he rubbed carefully.

"Got some blood on my hands," the vet said.

Funeral said nothing. Overhead a nighthawk flew. He zoomed down, wings braced; ear boomed. There was this sound, lonesome and strong, and then the hawklike bird was gone, moving swiftly into moonlight.

"What next?" Ringbone asked.

Funeral turned back toward the trail. His words came back over his shoulder. "Nothing we can do. We know where the bodies are. Tomorrow we can move them. They will keep for a day or so in this weather." They reached the lip of the trail. They stood there for a moment, looking down into the blackness of the coulee. "My slab will be filled to capacity."

"And more might be ahead," Ringbone Smith said ominously.

They got their broncs and rode out of the badlands, leaving the two dead men behind them. They unsaddled Gittler's horse, throwing the saddle and bridle and blanket into the brush, marking the spot in their memories, for they would either return for the gear, or send somebody after it.

Because of the narrowness of the trail, Ringbone Smith had to ride behind his friend, and the veterinarian wondered what thoughts tumbled through Funeral O'Neill's brain. But he asked no questions at this time. He had resolved to let his partner do the thinking and plotting out their course of action. But, of course, if he did not agree — then he would raise his voice in opposition. But, for now, he would allow the undertaker to be the boss.

They left the badlands and then the veteninary moved his horse even with that of Funeral O'Neill. They had hardly got into the area covered with sagebrush when the undertaker pulled his horse to a halt.

"Rider coming this way," he said tersely.

Ringbone stood on stirrups, squinting into the moonfilled distance, and then he settled down again, corpulent body thick between fork and cantle.

"Seems as though I should know that rider," he muttered. "From the way he sits his saddle; he seems familiar."

"Coming from the direction of town," Funeral said.

Ringbone's voice now held an excited edge.

"That's Millie Wetherford," he exclaimed.

And he was right. The rider did indeed prove to be Ed Burnett's fiancee. She was riding a big bay horse. They saw the moonlight glisten on steel, and Funeral raised his voice in recognition.

"O'Neill and Smith, Millie girl. Put that pistol away, woman."

She curbed in, her bronc rearing. His forehoofs pawed the thin air, then settled down. She pouched her pistol and her face was pale with excitement. She tried to talk, but, at first, no words would come.

"Calm down, woman," the undertaker soothed.

"Did you men know that Ed broke out of jail?"

Funeral O'Neill assured her that this knowledge was known to them. He then asked her some questions.

"Where are you going in such a rush, Millie?"

"I'm going out to call the farmers together. Ed is fighting for them and they can fight for him. Besides, he might have headed out to get them in a bunch, to ride against the Gardner gunmen."

Funeral looked at Ringbone. Even on the moonlight he could see the seriousness of his partner's glum face. If the farmers rode in a gun hung group against the Gardner gunmen . . . well, that was just what Gardner wanted. His men were gunmen, some were killers; the farmers were, for the most part, poor riflemen, even slower and worse with six-shooters. It would be massacre..nothing more.

He decided to change the subject. "Which direction did Ed go when he left town?" he asked.

She said, "Ed was supposed to head north. But I think he headed that way to throw the posse off his trail, then he would double around and go south – to meet the farmers and talk this over with them."

Ringbone Smith said, "Might be so."

Suddenly she asked, "Where have you two been?"

Funeral O'Neill told her about finding the corpse of Fred Gittler and the Gardner gunman. She was mystified. He realized, then, that Ed had told her nothing. Ed Burnett and Fred Gittler had kept their secret securely from her and from the farmers. He guessed that Mrs. Gittler knew about their secret. Her conversation, abrupt and jagged though it had been, had so informed the undertaker and veterinarian that her husband had confided in her.

"Wonder where Clint Gardner is?" Ringbone Smith asked.

"He rode with the posse," Millie frowned.

Funeral O'Neill asked, "And that fat gink – that Henderson fellow – who stays in the hotel?"

"He also rode with Dunlap and his posse."

Funeral merely nodded. Plans and half-plans were darting through his brain. Ringbone Smith mouthed a fresh peppermint. He winced a little and Funeral looked at him, wondering what had caused his grimace.

"Got a sour tooth. Some peppermints are sweeter than others. They hurt the tooth."

"Two things to do."

"What?"

"Either pull the tooth . . . or stop chewing those damned things. Well, Millie, reckon you'd best be on your way, and if you see Ed give him our regards and tell him to contact us through you."

"I'll do that . . . if I see him. Where are you two going?"

"Heading back for town, I reckon. We ain't got no call to ride out at our ages on such a cold night."

"You sound like an old man," she scoffed. "Why not ride with me?"

"Some other time," Funeral said.

She turned her horse and loped away. Soon the moonlight and the distance claimed her and she dropped from view.

Ringbone said, "She won't have no luck. Them farmers won't fight, and I don't blame them one bit."

"Give her something to do," Funeral said.

Ringbone made a noise crunching his peppermint. "Well, if Ed did hit north, where is he now, would you say off-hand?"

"He and Gittler were working together. We know that much for sure. So I figure he'd either swing around and head for the Gittler homestead to contact his friend, or else head for his homestead."

"From what we can gather," Ringbone said slowly, "Ed has until midnight to stake out his homestead, and unless he gets it staked out tonight, he loses his entry fee and his homestead rights. Is that it?"

"So it appears from here, Ringbone."

"Good thinking," Funeral said.

"Continue on, my friend."

Ringbone stabbed a sharp look at the undertaker. Funeral noticed the sharpness of that glance but said nothing.

"For once," Ringbone Smith murmured, "you said I did something right . . . Well, two men will try to keep him from staking out that homestead, and those two hombres will be Michael Henderson and Clint Gardner."

"Again, solid thinking."

Ringbone glanced at the moon. His next words were directed toward the Man there. "I'm going to die of shock. He's twice complimented me." He swung his gaze back to his partner. His big hands were crossed on his wide-topped saddlehorn. "These things being understood, looks like we got our work cut out for us, Funeral."

"Reckon so."

"We got to hold that homestead for Ed. Them two hellions will try to cut him off – keep him from getting his settlement-stakes down by midnight, which ain't far distance around the clock."

"So I figure."

"Missus Gittler could tell us more," Ringbone Smith said. "There are some ends that my mind ain't tied in yet."

"All clear to me," Funeral said. "I told you there was more than that editorial and the settlement of the farmers behind this. From the beginning, it looked bigger than that to me."

"You were right, Funeral."

Funeral rubbed his jaw thoughtfully. He needed a shave. His whiskers made rough sounds against his fingers.

"Gardner and Henderson might not have stuck it out with Dunlap's posse," the undertaker said. "That might have been just an excuse to get them out of town. They might have left the posse, doubled over to the homestead, and right now might be squatting there — waiting for Ed Burnett to ride into their guns."

"Reckon they figure we know about the homestead?"

"I don't know." Funeral gave this angle deep thought. "I doubt it, though. But they are tough men. They have killed to get this land, and they'll kill to keep it."

"They'd kill us as quick as a drunk could uncork a new bottle."

"They're wanted men, if this thing kicks back on them. The gallows will be waiting for them, and they'll fight until they are dead," Funeral said.

"You sound like you're worried,"

They were riding at a walk toward the distant bulk of Rising Butte. The wind moved in, rustling the sagebrush, and the wind was cold. Neither man noticed its chill, though; each fought and wrestled with his thoughts.

"This isn't going to be no grammar school picnic," Funeral O'Neill gravely pointed out. "They ain't kicking no fortune in the teeth."

"You still sound worried."

"If you want to know the truth, I am worried, Ringbone."

"Maybe you're worried about the trouble you'll face with the Law," Ringbone Smith taunted, the brim of his hat shielding his eyes.

"What are you driving at by that remark?"

"You smuggled a gun to Ed Burnett. You helped in a jail delivery. That is a harsh offense."

"Only three people know," the undertaker warned. "Me, you, and Ed. And if you breathe a word to Dunlap, I'm getting you on the slab – and with pleasure will I shoot the formalin in your veins, my sterling friend."

Ringbone smiled, mission accomplished. "I might tell . . . at that," he joked. Suddenly he became serious. "Do you figure somebody did away with old man Quinn, Funeral?"

"I sure do think he was murdered."

"Who did it?"

"Gardner, I figure."

"On what do you base that conjecture?"

"Never knew you knew such big words. I figure it this way. Quinn left the Tribune office for a bottle of beer for Old Press. Williams comes in, right after Quinn had left, and he slugs Old Press, but never got to kill him. So, he sets fire on the place, figuring it will burn Old Press, which it did not — thanks to us. Gardner wants the Tribune silenced. He wanted to make it look like he was fighting the Tribune because it was a newspaper against him. He wanted to get the public eye off his light with Ed, over the home entry."

"That sounds logical. Go on?"

"Well, Gardner is in the alley, and Williams, after setting the fire, after slugging Old Press, beats it down the alley. Well, along comes old man Quinn, beer bottle and all, but, from what I gather, he saw one thing — something he should not have seen."

"Like what, for instance?"

"I may be wrong, and this is all supposition — but I figure he came in just as Williams was doing his dirty work, and they had to kill him because of what he saw Williams doing."

"You think Gardner killed him?"

"I think so. Either him or Williams. They slugged him, killed him, then toted his body out to that coulee, heaving him overboard."

"That could have been done so easy, too," Ringbone said thoughtfully. "You lay a man belly or back-down in a low wagon, and throw a tarp over him – who is to know you're not hauling firewood, or groceries?"

"That's the deal, Ringbone."

Ringbone sucked a peppermint. "Only reason there was to kill my old friend," he said. "Him and me had many a bottle and cribbage board between us. I'm killing them that killed him, if I get the chance."

"You might get it . . . before sunrise, too."

"If Gardner did it, I gun him down."

Ringbone Smith had controlled anger in his voice. Funeral O'Neill knew his partner well, and he knew that a harsh desire for revenge was in the veterinarian who, usually, was a soft-spoken, good natured man.

"You get the corpse of Clint Gardner on my slab," Funeral O'Neill said tightly, "and I'll use my needle on him happily."

"And for free, too?"

"Gratis," the undertaker substantiated.

They had one more stop to make, and that was at the Fred Gittler home. The house was dark and silent. Only one dog came out barking at them. The other, for some reason, stayed in the sod shack. Funeral hoorayed the house and the woman came to the door. She had a rifle but she carried no lamp.

"Back again," the undertaker said. "Ringbone and I want to talk to you, my good woman, if you will so allow."

"Is it about – my husband?"

"Yes, somewhat so. More than that, though."

"Come in, sirs."

They went into the close air of the house. Darkness was heavy, settling in corners, laying over the furniture. She seated herself close to the window. From here she would watch the yard that lay clear in moonlight.

"My oldest boy," she said. "He is keeping guard in the back."

Funeral O'Neill leaned against the

wall, feeling the wall against his back. Ringbone Smith squatted, watching out the door. Because of the porch, moonlight could not reach him, he was dark and compact, a dark spot in surrounding darkness. He again let his partner do the talking.

Funeral told the woman about their finding her husband's body, and he told about their discovery of the dead Gardner's man, there in the canyon. She took it with a soft groan, nothing more. No tears. Funeral O'Neill got the impression that she had expected this; their other conversation had disclosed this to him, also. She made funeral arrangements. He said that he doubted if Gardner and Henderson would hit at her and her family. They had eliminated her husband; he had been their strongest opponent. He doubted if the range would stand for the two molesting a woman and her family, especially after that wife and family had lost the husband and father. She could go out with her wagon, if she so wanted, and recover the body. This she declined to do. The body would be safe until a wagon arrived to take her husband to town for burial. And Henderson and Gardner might sneak in, when she and her children were gone, and burn their home and buildings.

"Good thinking," Funeral encouraged.

He asked more questions, putting them in a low and what he hoped was a confidential tone of voice.

From somewhere back in the darkness a child sobbed. The sobbing had started when he had told about their finding Fred Gittler's ambush and his body.

The sobbing sounded as though it came from a young girl. Gittler had a lovely little daughter of five or six. Funeral O'Neill had seen the child a number of times, and his masculine heart had been warmed by her presence. Now she sobbed back there in the dark because her father had been murdered. The undertaker, a stern man of controlled emotions, a man who, because of his calling, had little if any personal feeling, now felt a hardness come into his throat.

He felt a hand touch his boots. The hand rested there. It was the hand of Ringbone Smith. And Funeral knew that his partner, too, was effected.

From the back room came the calm voice of a boy. "The coast is all clear, mother," he said.

His voice then choked. He, too, had heard the sad news brought by the partners. He was the man of the house now. He was about ten, Funeral figured. Fate was shoving a stern load off on youthful shoulders.

"Was Miss Millie here?" Ringbone asked.

"Yes, she was here. She was worried about Ed."

"She had just right to be worried," Funeral said. "What did she say?"

"She didn't stay but a minute, then she headed for the Swanson farm. I hope the farmers do not organize and move against Gardner. He'll – he'll – kill them, men. He wants to kill them, and if they move against him they'll do just what he wants them to do . . . get in a bunch and his killers will shoot them down."

"From what I understand," Funeral said, slowly, "Ed Burnett has not filed full claim on his homestead entry. Is that right?"

"You're not right, Mr. O'Neill."

Funeral had a moment of surprise. He had read the letters in Ed's desk, back in the Tribune composing room, and from them he had so gathered this information; now this woman said his assumptions had been false.

"Wherein, madam, do I err?"

She told him in terse words. With his homestead entry, Ed Burnett had also filed a mining claim. "A mining claim, you know, can be filed on a homestead, and it need not be filed by the man who owns the homestead rights."

Ringbone Smith cut in with, "Do I understand right, Mrs. Gittler? Let's put it this way: for the sake of clarity, I'll say I own a homestead — the entry is all proper, and the land is mine. Could Funeral, if he wanted, then file a mining claim, on my land?"

"Yes, unless you owned mineral rights."

Ringbone pursued it still further. "Then, even if I had wheat on my farm, and it was growing, Funeral could move in workers and rigs, and destroy my wheat working his mine?"

"Right."

Ringbone said, "Well, I'll be – " He checked himself in time. "Pardon me, Mrs. Gittler. But I learned something."

Funeral O'Neill now spoke. "So when Ed filed for homestead, he also filed on mining rights, as did your husband. Has Ed got his mining rights yet?"

"Not yet."

"Has he got his homestead entry in order, do you know?"

"He has that lined up. He has to make improvements – build a cabin, do some plowing. Fred has done this for him. Plowing, that is; no cabin, as yet. Fred was going to build the cabin next but now . . . "

There was a silence. The boy was sobbing now, too. Funeral waited respectfully, then asked, "Has Ed got his mining claim lined up?"

"He has his location stakes out. But the mining examiner from the Capitol will be here — tomorrow — to see the claim boundaries. And if Ed hasn't it staked out, if his claim is not filed on the property, then he does not get the mining rights, and they are what count — that is why Fred filed on this piece of land. Just for the mineral rights."

"Well, I'll be hanged,"exploded Ringbone Smith. "No wonder Gardner and Henderson moved so fast today. Sent Colt Hagen to kill Ed, so they could stake the claim; this backfired, and Ed got in jail. Then tried to burn his outfit to burn the papers in his desk. Wonder how come they never took them papers out when they set the fire, Funeral?"

"Probably never had time. They were pressed for time. As it was, according to our calculations, they were caught in the act by old man Quinn."

The woman listened.

Ringbone Smith had a hoarse voice. "And then they figured the building would burn, and the papers would naturally be burnt up, too. And there was Old Press, knocked cold, and they wanted to burn him, too."

"The dirty murderers," the mother said angrily. "I wish I were a man. I'd hunt them down . . ." She stopped suddenly.

"Don't think such thoughts," Funeral O'Neill said kindly.

"Why not? Stanley killed my husband. Stanley worked for Gardner. Then Gardner indirectly murdered my husband."

"Henderson is in on this too," Ringbone reminded.

"I could kill that fat devil, too."

Funeral said, "I want to talk to your son," and he moved across the dark room. He batted his shins on the low center-table but, despite the pain, he did not cry out. He came into a bedroom. The boy was beside the window.

"Over here, Mr. O'Neill."

Funeral put his arm around the thin shoulders. "Son," he said, "take your mother out in the wagon, and get your father's body. I'm afraid that if she sits here, and if she thinks too much, she might do something she shouldn't do."

"Like ride for the Gardner outfit, with a rifle?"

"Yes, son."

"I'll get her to go with me," the boy said. "We got a harnessed team in the barn, just for an emergency."

"Do that, Freddie boy."

A small hand came up, fumbled, found his, pressed his. And a boyish voice, choked with sobs, spoke and said, "What if they sneak in . . . burn our property?"

"They won't do that, Freddie. Ringbone and I will see to that. Your house will be just like it is when you get back."

The pressure increased. The hand dropped.

"I wonder if I can ever thank you and Mr. Smith enough, Funeral."

"You have one way, Freddie?"

"And that?"

"When you grow up, be a good strong

man. Add to your community and your family, and make you mother proud of you, like she is proud of your daddy."

"I'll do that, Mr. O'Neill."

Funeral O'Neill and his partner helped the widow get the rig moving. They harnessed the team to the flat-bottom wagon while the boy and his mother and sister took out blankets and laid on the wagon's bed. They also took a tarp. Then Funeral gave the widow explicit direction as to the location of her husband's body. Soon the rig rolled into the moonlight, wheels making sloppy sounds in the mud. It had not been a happy occasion. Funeral remembered tackling Fred Gittler, back there in the alley, and he remembered knocking the man out. Gittler had been merely on a reconnaisance trip, sizing up the situation.

He was sure of that, now. When he had tackled the man, he had not known Gittler's true position in this trouble; he knew this now, of course. The wagon rolled into the night and became lost from view and beyond the perimeter of sound.

"A terrible thing for a wife to have to do," Ringbone Smith intoned. He dug in his slicker pocket for a peppermint. "Well, we learned something, huh, Funeral?"

"We sure did."

"Wonder where Ed Burnett is?"

"Been wondering where he is."

"What would you do . . . if you were in his boots?"

"I'd stay single and not get married, like he contemplates."

Funeral O'Neill grimaced sourly. "What a laughable bit of humor," he said. "I'm serious, horse doctor."

They stood in the shadow of the porch. Impatience was in each of them, driving them to physical action, but they kept these stirrings locked tightly. The entire case — this whole deal — was now clear to them. What few conflicts there had been had been cleared by the words of Fred Gittler's widow.

And the savage brutality of Clint Gardner and Michael Henderson was now openly apparent.

Ringbone Smith was silent for some time. "When the posse left town, it headed north, so Millie said. But Ed's homestead is not north, it is south. And he has to have this location notice on it when the Territorial Mining Examiner comes in the morning to check the validity of his claim."

"Right."

"Then, if I were Ed, I would swing north, ride in a big circle, and head south – this way, I'd throw the posse way off. Dunlap would have no way of knowing that Ed has filed a mining claim on the strip, would he?"

Funeral considered that for a brief clock-tick. "No, I don't think so," he finally said, and then he added, I'm sure he doesn't know."

"Well, he'll head north, then, thinkin' Ed Burnett has headed for the Canadian Line, and Ed will dodge the posse and swing south, I figure. Besides, he might want to talk to us, you know."

"But he doesn't realize we know about

his mining claim and about the ore that is causing all this death and trouble."

"Well, that is right. But we can't forget that Ed is a fugitive from justice, Funeral."

"He might turn into a dead fugitive," Funeral O'Neill said, "if he runs into the guns of this fat Henderson stiff and Clint Gardner."

"Which would be the worse? Death under their guns . . . or marriage?"

"You aren't a bit funny," the undertaker growled. "Then you figure Ed would head out for his homestead?"

"That I do."

"And do you figure he would stop in and look to see if he could talk to Fred Gittler?"

"He might."

"They were partners, remember?"

"He won't know Gittler is dead, unless he takes the badland short-cut and happens to meet the widow and her children in that wagon."

"That's right."

"Wonder if he will get his farmers

out to fight the Gardner killers? Wonder what luck, if any, Millie is having?"

"Hope she has none. One widow at a time is enough for this basin."

Ringbone Smith brushed the dust off a peppermint he had in his vest pocket. He crammed it into this wide mouth and laid it on the right side of his cheek so he could talk around it.

"What about Henderson, and Gardner?" he asked.

"What about them?"

"What would they do?"

"Why don't you answer that?"

"Your turn," Ringbone Smith said. "I answered the last questions."

Funeral O'Neill's forehead became grooved by a frown. "If I were in the boots of Henderson and Gardner, I would make a good pretense of riding with Dunlap's posse, and, all the time, I would be thinking that Ed Burnett had headed north only to throw the Law off his trail, and that he would turn south to his mining-claim."

"And then what?"

"They would get out of town with the posse, then quit it without anybody seeing them, and circle around and guard that strip of ore."

"Then they should be watching that ledge right now, by those tokens, eh, Funeral?"

"Depends of how far they rode with the posse. They would ride for some time and distance, to make it look like they were in earnest. That mining claim examiner is not due until about noon on the stage, you know."

"Wonder how much time we have spent since we left town?"

"Oh, not too long. A couple of hours, maybe."

"Daylight ain't far off," Ringbone said. "We got one thing to do first, then, huh?"

"Yes, I think so."

"Get hold of Ed Burnett and get him out of this fight. Keep him in cold storage until the trouble is over. They have already killed Fred Gittler to get his land and mining rights. The next man they want to get out of circulation is one named Ed Burnett. Sure lucky you turned Ed out of jail."

"They'd have killed him. Shot him down like a goldfish in a bowl. Those letters in his desk tipped me off."

"We got to get hold of Ed."

Funeral O'Neill was peering down the road that led to Boxelder. "Seems to me," he said, "that a rider is coming this way."

"Looks that way. Now who could he be?"

The rider was loping toward the building, angling through the sagebrush. Moonlight was not clear enough to prove his identity; distance, too, was against them.

"He sets a saddle danged familiar," the veterinarian said.

Funeral said, slowly, "Unless I'm plumb cockeyed, friend, that rider should be nobody but Ed Burnett."

Ringbone Smith sucked in a savage breath. "And that is who it is, too – I can see for sure, now that he is closer.

And it is only logical he head for this spread, anyway."

"He rides to see his friend, Fred Gittler," the undertaker said. "Good luck we tied our broncs in the shadow of the barn. He can't see them because they are on the high side of the barn. There goes the dog, out barking at him. The dogs know him. See, he called to him, and he stopped barking."

"What are we going to do?"

"We are going to make a prisoner out of Ed Burnett," Funeral said. "Then he can't get killed and leave Millie a widow even before they get married."

"Good idea."

They pulled back into the darkness of the house. Ringbone crossed the room, took out his .45, and squatted, back to the wall. Funeral stood beside the door, back to the wall, also. This way, when Ed Burnett entered, one would be behind him, the other ahead of him.

"I'll jab a gun in his pretty little back," the undertaker grunted.

And this he eventually did. They heard

Ed call out, "Hello, the house," and then, on receiving no answer, the publisher dismounted, strode across the porch, knocked on the door. Again, no reply, so he entered, six-shooter in his hand. And then he froze as the round barrel of Funeral's .45 dug into his back.

"Drop that short-gun, Ed Burnett, and put up your hands."

There was a moment of awesome silence. Across the room, Ringbone Smith got to his boots, a shadow moving in shadows.

"This is Ringbone Smith and Funeral O'Neill, Ed Burnett. Did we hear your gun drop to the floor, publisher?"

"No."

"Then, drop it!" Ringbone's voice was thick with hard authority. "You're riding for trouble, young man."

Then, the fingers opened. The big .45 clattered to the floor.

"That's better," Funeral O'Neill said. "Ringbone, light the lamp, huh?"

"All right, boss."

Soon the yellow rays of the kerosene

lamp were fighting back the dark shadows of the room. Lamplight glistened on the stern young face of Ed Burnett.

"Why stick a gun in my back?" the publisher demanded.

Funeral O'Neill answered with, "We want to keep you in one piece . . . for the prettiest little girl in the basin. Gittler is dead, boy."

"Fred Gittler . . . dead?"

Funeral nodded, eyes somber. Ringbone Smith sat at the table, hands cupped around his head as he watched. Again, he let his partner do the talking.

"He was well, when I last saw him," Ed said.

Funeral shook his gaunt head. "They killed him. Stanley – that Gardner man – waylaid him and bushwhacked him, out in the badlands. On the short cut."

"My God, men. His wife – children – "

Funeral said, "They have gone to pick up the body. Had you taken the short-cut, you'd have met them. They aim to kill you next, Ed."

"I'll be hard to kill."

Again the undertaker shook his dour head in sour manner. "A bullet cares not who it kills," he intoned. "They are going to storm your homestead entry. We know all about that Strip, young man. Why didn't you tell us before?"

"How did you find out?"

"From correspondence in your desk. From raiding Henderson's hotel room. Yes, and from Mrs. Gittler, God bless her patient soul."

"Why didn't you tell us?" Ringbone Smith asked. "Damn it, man, aren't we your friends?"

Ed Burnett's face assumed a look of regret. His eyes moved from one man to the other. He had dropped his hands now. His .45 still lay on the floor. He lifted his eyes to the veterinarian sitting at the homemade table.

"I never thought of it, to be truthful. I never knew that Gardner would find out that strip contained chromite. I'd never have known about the chromite had not Gittler told me. Gittler is no farmer. He is — or *was,* rather — a geologist."

"You should have told us," Ringbone Smith scolded mildly.

Ed Burnett shrugged. "They'll try to tear down my claim notice. And the mining-claim examiner is coming into town today. I got to get to my claim — fight them off — I got to."

"No," Ringbone said.

Funeral shook his head again.

"We are," Funeral said.

Ed Burnett laughed throatily. "You're not fighting this man's battles, you two. I'll get my gun and — "

He acted, then.

He squatted, grabbing for his gun. But the boot of Funeral O'Neill came shashing in, kicking the gun to one side. Ed Burnett straightened. Then, without warning, his knees became weak. His eyes rolled. And he pitched to the floor on his belly. He did not move.

Lamplight glistened on the upraised .45 in the hand of Funeral O'Neill.

Ringbone Smith, who had started to leave his chair, settled down and something akin to admiration fired its way across his eyes, giving his face a satanic appearance.

"You hit just right, Funeral."

Funeral O'Neill grinned with lazy indifference. "I have lots of practice lately," he intoned dryly. "I had to hit a little harder because his rain-helmet deflected the blow somewhat."

Ringbone moved over, squatted. He looked like a human bear, there in the yellow lamplight. His hand went under the unconscious man's shirt. He looked down, taking his count. Then he regained his feet.

"Heart as steady as a steam motor. What do we do with junior, undertaker?"

"Tie him up and put him in the side room."

"Lock him in there?"

Funeral shook his head. Although he looked calm, he was raw inside. To slug a man competently, without braking his skull or without hitting too easily, is a difficult feat, but apparently he had mastered it somewhat adequately.

"There's a window there, so no use locking him in. People are odd things, Ringbone. When they build a house they put on great enormous locks and all the time, to gain entry, all a man has to do is boot his way through a window pane, about an eighth of an inch thick."

"Which makes the locks useless," the veterinarian grunted, "and the subject is not one for present conversation, either. Do I drag carcass, or do you?"

"I slug him. You drag him."

"I might slip my sacroiliac."

"Let it pop, Grandpa."

Ringbone Smith got both legs belonging to Ed Burnett, put a boot under each elbow, then pulled the man into the side room, looking for all the world like a horse laboring between shafts.

This room was evidently the bedroom belonging to the parents. They put the unconscious publisher on the bed and then pulled the spread out from under him with a hard and quick jerk.

"What we going to do with that bedspread?" Ringbone asked.

"*We* aren't going to do anything with it," Funeral O'Neill said. "*You* are going to tie his hands and feet."

"Tear it, you mean?"

"Yes, rip it into pieces."

Ringbone Smith looked at the bedspread. It was a new one. Pink and with a trim of lace.

"Mrs. Gittler might not like this."

"We'll get her another one, a better one."

"We'll do that." The veterinarian smiled. The spread was tough. He had to start the rips by cutting the edges with his pocket-knife. But within a few minutes he had the publisher tied hand and foot. Ed Burnett was still sleeping mouth sagging. Funeral glanced into his mouth.

"Wish I had his teeth," the undertaker said woefully.

Ringbone said, "What is next?"

"We leave him here, of course. Now where do you suppose those two gentlemen of the pistol trail are located at this moment?"

"Who do you mean?"

"Henderson and Gardner, of course."

"Hell, that's an easy one. They'll head for that claim to keep Ed Burnett off it, they will."

"I think so too," Funeral said.

They went outside. Soon dawn would be on the land. They looked at the ridge wherein lay the chromite ore.

Black and ugly, discernible in the coming of day, the strip of igneous rock stretched across the two homesteads, marring the base of high Rising Butte, which soon would be bathed with sunrise because of its high altitude. About a mile in length, this heat-warped strip rose and pitched, sometimes getting about ten feet above the soil, sometimes sinking beneath the soil and hiding itself. It was a harsh black coiling snake, lying there on the fertile breast of the Montana prairie, and it had lain thus for millions of years, awaiting the coming of two-legged greedy man to unlock its magnificent secret.

Over it had walked and had ridden

many men, some races now gone beyond the scope of anthropology and time, dead and unknown against the millions of millions of years, lost in the shuffle of ice and dirt and heat and frigid cold. Sioux and Gros Ventres had sat on it, ridden across it. Red men had not wanted its treasure, for the redmen had been practical, and a man cannot eat steel or gold. Buffalo had thundered across it by the thousands, and red arrows had felled them, turning them to jerky and tanning their hides for teepees and quivers and rawhide *lassos.* A man could eat buffalo meat, the hide of buffalo kept man warm. Rock was cold and rock was useless, except to throw in search of game, or in self defense.

And so, the ledge had lain dormant.

Then, too, there had been the black wolf, and he had gone south to escape the terrible winter to the north, and the black wolf had sat there on that ledge, belly gaunt and ribs showing through his shaggy coat. And he had raised his terrible hungry jowls and the mouth had opened slightly, and the black timber wolf had howled – and animals had shivered and fled. The deer had leaped from his thicket, the buffalo had stormed to a safe distance, and the jackrabbit had leaped from his hiding place, there in the tall sagebrush.

The wolf was gone, too.

Now men – two legged creatures – hungry for gold, for fame, fought over this ledge, for science had unlocked its treasure.

Funeral O'Neill swung his mind from such speculations and he looked at his partner, who also was looking toward Rising Butte.

"We hide in the brush along the Strip," the undertaker said. "I doubt if they have had time to make the loop yet, and reach their destination."

"Wonder where they are?" the undertaker said.

The Boxelder partners had guessed correctly when they had allowed that Michael Henderson and cowman Clint Gardner would not ride very far, or very long, with the posse lead by Sheriff Dunlap — the posse that was out to hunt down Ed Burnett. For the posse headed north. And Gardner and Henderson, who knew things that the sheriff and the gun-riders did not know, knew full well that when Ed Burnett had headed north out of Boxelder, he had done this only to throw the posse and sheriff onto a cold trail.

For Ed Burnett's mining-claim was south of town, not north.

But they dared not leave too soon, for that might evoke suspicion against them. About a mile out of town, Henderson managed to find his horse next to that of Clint Gardner, there on the edge of the passe.

He leaned low in saddle.

"How do you suppose Ed Burnett got hold of a .45?"

"From O'Neill, of course."

Henderson had leaned even closer to his companion in crime. "What gets me is this: Funeral O'Neill has openly advocated that Ed Burnett stay in jail until the inquest in the morning finds him guilty or turns him loose. Then, all of a sudden, that damned undertaker changes his mind, and smuggles Burnett a gun. That ain't logical to me, Clint."

"Is to me."

"In what way."

Gardner glanced around, looking at the scattered riders there in the Montana moonlight. "Reckon nobody can hear us, huh?"

"They can't. Too far away."

"I don't understand that myself. Not one bit, Henderson. But maybe he never smuggled that gun to Burnett."

"If he didn't, who did?"

"Could have been smuggled in by Burnett's woman."

Henderson nodded, moonlight etching his huge figure. He rode his saddle like a veteran. He had been scared in Texas and had gone to school there for a year or so, majoring in geology. He had a wife and three boys in El Paso. He had something else, too – greed. Greed was deep in the marrow of his big bones.

Greed poisoned and tinted his brain. He had heard about the chromite ledge through a confidential report filed by an engineer in his office.

Needless to say, the head of the engineering firm never saw the report. Henderson had headed west with it. A fortune was there . . . for the taking . . . But Fred Gittler had beat him to the chromite strip. And Gittler had informed his friend, Ed Burnett, and now, between the two of them, they had the Strip sewed up tightly.

So Henderson had turned to the guns of Clint Gardner. Gardner would do two things at one time, bring around two goals. He would get wealthy off chromite, and, by the same struggle, rid the range of farmers. And, when the time came, he might even get rid of one Michael Henderson.

These thoughts were with the big cowman. Henderson and he had talked it over; the time had come to get rid of Fred Gittler. Stanley would see to that. Then, money in his pocket,

Stanley would drift out, and Gittler would be dead behind him. Gittler's wife . . . she was just a woman, easy to defeat. Nothing to worry about. He wondered: Has Stanley pulled off the job yet. Things were moving fast. Black shadows, there across the moonlight; shadows dancing, moving, beckoning. The only thing that had gone wrong was the failure to burn down the Tribune office and its confidential papers. Yes, and the plot to kill Ed Burnett, there in his cell. Those two things, vital and necessary, had not come through as he had planned.

Well, Burnett was only human. One bullet, placed in the right spot of his anatomy. One bullet . . .

And old man Quinn . . . Old fool, blundering along, beer bottle in his hand. They had been lucky they had got his body out of town without anybody seeing them. He dismissed the memory from his mind. His attention soared over and focused on two men: Undertaker

Funeral O'Neill and Ringbone Smith. They had broken up his plans. They had kept the print-shop from burning to the ground.

Henderson said, "Wonder who slugged me in my hotel room?"

"I don't know who it was, but I wonder *why?*"

"Nothing was missing from my room," Michael Henderson said. "Hell, they'll never catch this Burnett son. You can't track a skunk in the moonlight, not when the ground is sopping wet, too."

"Sure right there," Gardner grunted.

Within a half hour, Sheriff Dunlap waved them into a group. They sat heaving horses under the moon. Moonlight glistened on polished silver trappings, saddles creaked under the rise of heaving ribs and a horse rolled the cricket in the port of his bit. Beyond them was the sagebrush – gray and silver and golden under the moon – and the smell of damp sage, too, was in the slow air, turning and rolling and filling a man's nostrils. And, beyond

BR18

the moonlight, to the north, was the slow rise of the foothills, dim plunging shadows, nothing more.

Sheriff Dunlap spoke in a thick voice. Importance was a sterling weight on his narrowed shoulders, and this put the solid note in his words. They would split up and comb the breaks that twisted and became the foothills. Their quarry, from all indications, was skipping the country. He was heading for Canada and by morning, unless he were stopped or killed or captured, he was out in Canada. Dunlap rattled off names. Four men rode in a body. Henderson and Gardner saw to it that they were in different groups; they had their plan made, each knew his part. If they were assigned to the same group, and they turned broncs and deserted, then they would be missed immediately – two from four leaves a big hole. But, with each in a different group, they could pull out, and association would not tie them together – one from four leaves not such a large vacancy.

"Spread out and miss nothing." Sheriff Dunlap was savage. His authority had been seized, mangled, thrown back into his face, and the blood was on his lips. A man had broken out of his jail. He had slugged the deputy and had shot down a Gardner man. The latter incident, though, did not bother Sheriff Dunlap. He had little, if any use, for Clint Gardner.

"Shoot to kill?" a man asked.

"Shoot to kill," the lawman repeated.

This did not sit well with the posse. Almost all of them liked Ed Burnett. Some even called him *friend.* There had been lots of free whiskey passing around when the posse had left Boxelder. The amount of whiskey decreased in direct ratio to the distance traveled. Now there was very little whiskey, if any. They would not kill Ed Burnett. Dunlap knew this, though, and pretended he was not aware of this fact. Clint Gardner knew this, also. Gardner knew he and Henderson would not be the only riders to desert.

So they swung out, riding in groups of four, and Dunlap had the center, heading into the hills. Within twenty minutes, a rider came up to Clint Gardner, who sat his bronc in the shadow of a cottonwood tree, there in a wide coulee, his break already made.

Michael Henderson said, "Your sheriff is a fool, Gardner."

"That is why we elected him," Gardner said. He turned his horse. "Now to get to that claim, tear down his location notices, and post our own. Or has he only one location notice posted?"

"Just one, for the law only needs one."

"He has the paper in that rock monument he built, huh?"

"He has it there. In a Prince Albert tobacco can. The law says one notice has to be posted on the mining-claim."

"And we abide all the time by the law," Gardner said and grinned.

Henderson caught the jest. "All the time," he repeated.

Clint Gardner neckreined his bronc

and pointed his south, and the horse carrying Michael Henderson followed suit. Henderson leaned from saddle.

"Burnett is not giving up that claim," he said. "He'll not ride north. He'll swing around and contact two men, I think."

"And they?"

"The vet, and the undertaker."

Clint Gardner's nod was short. "I think so, too. Look at it this way . . . Ed Burnett won't be in town when that mining-claim boss comes in. Ed can't be in town, and if he is caught, he goes to the clink. Anyway, either way, he won't be able to contact this mining-claim examiner."

"Not unless he sneaked around and met him in the sagebrush, while the man was riding out to the Strip."

Again, Gardner shook his head. "No can do . . . The man won't leave town. He'd have no call to ride out of town unless he got called out to see a mine. If Burnett doesn't contact him, then he stays the afternoon in Boxelder, and heads out tomorrow morning, because he doesn't ride out looking at claims . . . unless somebody asks him to."

Henderson nodded. "Well, he'll be asked, and the gent doing the asking will be either you or me, huh?"

"Right."

"And the claim notices, posted on each of these claims – on Burnett's and on Gittler's – will read not their names, but yours and mine, huh, Gardner?"

"Right, friend."

Henderson pursed the subject even further. "One of us will stand guard while the other brings out this mining man. Then nobody can sneak in and change our location notices. That might happen if both of us ride back to town after posting our claims. You ride back to town. I'll watch the claims."

"Good deal," Gardner said.

Henderson looked at his partner. "We're all set, then?"

"I got our claim notices in my pocket. We signed them down in your hotel room. All we got to do is get their notices out of those monuments, put up our notices, and then see nobody changes ours, fellow."

"Good."

They rode for some time in silence. They kept their horses at a lope. Not a fast gallop but a long, swinging stride that could and did cover miles swiftly and in short time. They forded Boxelder Creek, the sky beginning to show sunrise to the east.

There was enough light to show the spraying of the cold water as their broncs hit the creek at Boney Crossing. Their horses wanted a drink but they drove them on, keeping tight reins. They came out on the far gravel-heavy bank and headed across the rolling hills toward the chromite strip. Both had his thoughts. Their thoughts were centered around the same point – money. This chromite was worth money. Big money, too, maybe in the millions. This would entirely revolutionize this community.

Miners and mining equipment would be moved in.

There would be explosions in the

earth, and spur would be run out from the prospective that railroad would go through this area, and the ore would be shipped out, probably south to Denver, down in Colorado. So dreamed the cowman named Clint Gardner. And so dreamed the man named Michael Henderson. They had killed for this strip of chromite. They would kill again, if necessary, to gain it, to hold it.

They swung around the toe of the badlands. Both thought of Stanley and Fred Gittler. Gardner said, "Stanley is on his way out. He never misses."

"There's Gittler's spread," the other man said. "The cow is bawling. She wants to be milked and turned loose. The calf is bawling, too. He wants milk. Nobody stirring."

Gardner said, "Don't ride that direction. It would bring you into rifle range from that house, and somebody might indentify me." His grin was rough and ugly. "And these farmers don't cotton to a gink named Clint Gardner."

So, accordingly, they swung wide of the Gittler homestead. Ahead of them was the ugly bleak strip of chromite ore. Brush ran out, thick and, in some places, as high as a man's head. The rise of the ledge held run-off water each spring and, whenever it rained, water was banked behind the rocky dike. Therefore the brush grew high and thick.

They dropped into a coulee and rode along it, and the coulee pinched out as it neared the Strip. They came to a clump of service-berry bushes and here Gardner, who was riding the point, drew in his horse.

"Good place to tie our cayusss," he said. "The rock monument built by Ed Burnett is due south of here."

"How far?"

"What's the matter with your voice?"

"Matter . . . with my voice? Nothing, of course."

Gardner tied his bronc to a thick branch, smile plainly visible. "You kinda got squeaky there on the word *far,*" he jibed. "Could it be that your belly is cold, Henderson?"

Henderson did not look at him. He was intent an the task of tying his bronc. His voice was natural when he said, "Not mine, friend, not mine. Maybe yours, huh?" He slid his rifle from its saddle-holster.

"Not mine," Gardner assured.

They moved through the brush, carrying their rifles, and they went along a trail that wound through the high underbrush. Gardner was in the lead. He did not like taking the lead. He did not trust Henderson. But there was not space enough for two men to walk abreast.

They came to the edge of the clearing. Before them lay their fortune – a dark unyielding strip of ore. Now Henderson had drawn even with Gardner.

They squatted there and Henderson said, "That's his monument – yonderly there – about a hundred feet or so out there?"

"That is it."

Henderson wet his lips but his tongue

was dry. He looked at the rock monument, It was about five feet tall. It was made of boulders. It marked the corner of Ed Burnett's claim — the northwest corner. Other monuments, all made of rock, but all three smaller than this one, marked the other three corners of the mining-claim. The taller monument, by law and custom, contained the claim-notice. By law, that notice had to be cached in this taller monument. Usually miners and prospectors put their claim notices in tobacco cans to keep rain and sun from wetting them or parching them. For rain could drip down through the rocks and the sun was an errant fellow, many times peeping into the monument, despite the rocks.

Henderson said, "Wonder if we are alone?"

"Maybe we should scout, huh?"

"I'll take the west brush," Henderson said.

They went into the brush. Both were gone almost half an hour. By this time, dawn had changed and had become strong daylight. Henderson was the first to return. Within a few minutes, his partner came out of the brush, rifle in hand.

"Anything or anybody?" Henderson asked.

"Nobody. And you."

"And not a thing man – or beast – did I see. Oh, yes, one cottontail rabbit." Gardner smiled grimly. "He doesn't count." He looked at the monument. "Well, here goes, man. Cover me from the brush?"

"Sure thing, partner."

Gardner said, "And if I get jumped, shoot to kill," and then openly he walked from the brush, heading for the rock monument.

Clint Gardner's boots made noises on the flinty ledge. He was cold inside, for a rifle was on him, and the man behind that rifle was greedy. But the claim notice had been made out in two names, not one – Clinton Gardner and Michael Henderson. And if Henderson ambushed him, the claim would do him no good, for two signatures were on it.

If Henderson killed him, he would have to file another claim. That detailed drawing up a new paper, a new claim-notice.

Gardner put these thoughts aside. He came to the monument. He began tearing it down, rolling rocks off the top, for he figured the claim-notice filed by Burnett would be about in the middle of the monument. But he had to work down to get at it.

Rocks rolled down. They were not big rocks. They were about a foot and less in diameter, except for the base rocks – these were bigger. The rocks bounced, made sounds, rolled, stopped.

Gardner worked, sweat coming on him. From the brush, Henderson watched. Henderson had small, beady eyes. He, too, had a film of sweat on him, but it was cold sweat. Greed was in him, firing his blood, giving his eyes an evil and ugly slant that, normally, they did not have.

His fingers, clutching his rifle, were solid, though.

Ringbone Smith and Funeral O'Neill had seen the Circle S pair scout through the brush. They had been hidden in the boulders, up on the slope; below them, every movement was clear. They had darted down the slope, moving from rock to rock, screened by the boulders, and now Ringbone Smith was behind Michael Henderson, and Funeral O'Neill was in the brush, about a hundred yards from his partner, and Funeral was watching Clint Gardner.

The mortician had his .30-30 Winchester. He had some thoughts, too – disturbing thoughts. First, he was thinking of Ed Burnett, tied back there in the cabin. It had been some time about an hour or so – since he and his partner had tied down the young printer. Ed would be mad at him. He had buffaloed him and knocked him cold. But he dismissed this thought from his mind; it had little, if any purpose. He kept thinking, though, of pretty Millie Wetherford. And the farmers. If she got the farmers organized, if they rode with their rifles – He did not like this thought. Some of them would die — and die violent deaths — if they were fool hardy enough to ride against the Circle S gunmen.

By this time, though, Mrs. Gittler would probably have arrived in town with the body of her husband, and her story would wing across the rangelands, moving with the speed that only gossip can attain.

The brutality of her tale, corroborated by the bodies of her husband and the gunman, Stanley, would congeal this range into two definite camps, one favoring the cowmen, the other favoring the hoemen. Funeral realized that two men had to be taken out of circulation, and taken out fast and convincingly, and those two men were Michael Henderson and Clint Gardner.

And here was Gardner, tearing down the monument. Funeral let him work. His plan called that he step out, rifle raised, after Gardner had posted his own claim notice, and had destroyed that belonging to Ed Burnett. Then, when Gardner was again rebuilding this rock monument, he, Funeral O'Neill, would place him under arrest . . . a citizen arrest.

They had agreed upon a signal. When Funeral moved out, Ringbone would have his rifle in the back of Michael Henderson, and he would call to his partner, telling Funeral that no gun would boom and kill him from the brush.

Now, throat dry, Funeral O'Neill awaited this signal.

There was only one sound, and this was made by the boulders being dislodged from the monument and tumbling to the ground. They hit each other and made sharp sounds. Funeral wondered if something had gone wrong. By now, Ringbone Smith should have hollered out. Had Henderson heard Ringbone, and had he made him captive? Funeral dismissed this thought, also. Had Henderson captured his partner, there would have been a scuffle, possibly a shot or so, and both he and Clint Gardner would have heard the sounds, and been warned.

What was wrong with Ringbone Smith, and what was holding him up?

There was nothing wrong with the veterinarian.

The trouble was all in Funeral O'Neill: he was too raw-nerved, too impetious. Ringbone Smith was a Blackfoot in the brush, and he could move with the stealth and agility of a Blackfoot brave, and he showed this now. He came in behind Michael Henderson and he did it so silently the man never knew there was another human in the brush. Ringbone Smith paused, rifle stuck out in front of him ahead of him about thirty feet was Henderson, squatting on his thick haunches, watching his partner destroy the rock monument. Ringbone grinned, and, without warning, lifted his voice in a high-pitched yell.

"I got Henderson, partner!"

That yell, blood-curdling and shrill, did many things. It brought Henderson to his feet, made him turn on wooden

BR19

knees, and it brought fear to him. this time, though, the vet, despite his size and slowness, had covered the distance separating him from Henderson. His rifle barrel was against the man's spine.

"Watch that rifle of yours, Henderson!"

Henderson froze, rifle half raised. The barrel was cold and demanding against his back. He glanced at Clint Gardner. Gardner, at the sound of the yell, had turned and now he stood flat-footed and still, but was not looking toward him and Ringbone Smith.

He was watching another man, and Henderson recognized Funeral O'Neill. For a moment, doubt and despair was in Henderson. But these were laced immediately by tough hardness, a strong vigilance.

"Get ahead," Ringbone Smith said. "Move into the clearing."

Henderson said, "All right, but don't fire, man. "You'll break my spine in two!"

His voice was far away, dim against the dawn.

They went forward, going along the trail, and Ringbone glanced at Funeral, who had his rifle on Clint Gardner.

"Don't reach for that rifle, Gardner, or I'll shoot and shoot to kill, savvy?"

The mortician's voice held a note of stern warning. He had his rifle up, but not to his shoulder.

One move from Gardner, the butt of the rifle would move upward, and stock would hit his shoulder, and his eyes would find quick sights. Gardner was aware of this, and he glanced at Michael Henderson, who still held his rifle, but who had the rifle of Ringbone Smith in his back.

He cursed Henderson with savage and short intensity. He called him about six names. None was complimentary. There was this moment and the whole thing was a scene frozen by the ice of surprise, this holding the four of them in ugly tableau. One move, one word, and the ice would crack, broken by the stabbing spit of rifles, and each man there was aware of this face.

Ringbone Smith it was who made the error that turned loose the guns.

He did not know that Michael Henderson had, for four years, been a private in the army, and he did not know then that the worse thing he could have done was hold the rifle against the man's back.

Later, he found out he should have not touched the man with the rifle, but he should have stood a few feet behind him, leaving a space of a foot or so – possibly more – between the end of the rifle's barrel and the back of Michael Henderson.

Henderson had been trained well. One facet of this training had consisted of ways to get out from under a rifle. He had been trained not to move in close and hold a rifle directly against a man's back. For a man can turn suddenly, the rifle barrel going past him, sliding off his back as he turned, and he can come up with his own rifle or pistol. Henderson and other privates had practiced this manoeuvre for hours, and now this came back to him with strong remembrance.

"Drop your rifle and — "

Henderson moved, then, and his movement broke the ice, smashing it into a million crackling wrinkles. He turned to his right and Ringbone Smith, who had some weight on the rifle, moved ahead, and Henderson, in turning, grabbed the rifle by the barrel, jerking on it with a savage hardness. His training had stood him in good stead. He did not even drop his rifle. He used his free hand, and he sent Ringbone Smith off balance, and then his scream was wild with triumph.

"Get your rifle, Gardner!"

Henderson's words were not needed. Already Clint Gardner was making his play, and he was scooping his short-gun out of its holster. He did not move toward his rifle. His pistol was the closest, and it was the fastest. So, crouched and tough, he lifted his weapon, and his eyes were brittle and full of hope, now.

Things happened now with great rapidity. Funeral O'Neill, seeing he was trapped, turned his rifle first on Henderson, for Henderson was lifting his own .30-30, bringing it up to his shoulder. One glance showed Ringbone Smith, sprawled on the ground; but he, too, still held his weapon.

Funeral O'Neill shot first at Henderson. He shot as rapidly as he could, and all the time he expected the bullet of Clint Gardner to hit him. Gardner, he knew, could handle a .45, and he could handle the gun with great and deadly efficiency. There was in him, too, an anger against his partner.

But this anger, when placed against the duress of the moment, was of no consequence – a fleeting fancy, nothing more. He felt his rifle stock move back. He saw Henderson falter, and then Ringbone Smith, swinging his rifle, holding onto the stock, hit Henderson across the shins. The stock broke with a loud crackling sound. Henderson went down, legs moved from under him. He landed on his face, and Funeral then swung the rifle toward Clint Gardner, knowing all the time Gardner had him beaten.

But Clint Gardner did not fire. He was bent at the knees, his gun hanging in his hand, the barrel pointing downward. His head was bent, too, his neck at a sharp angle. Still, Funeral O'Neill could see his face. And his face was terrible, for the bullet had hit him on the side of the head, killing him in his tracks. And then, he was on the ground.

Funeral turned, then. He thought, somebody sure saved my life, and then he heard the crack of the rifle, up there on the slope about a hundred yards away. He saw the hang of powdersmoke in the rocks. He saw this, and heard this, and he felt light suddenly, for that rifle had given him a reprieve. He was still alive, and, by all rights, he should have been dead now, dead under the short-gun of Clint Gardner.

Henderson sobbed, lying now on his side. Ringbone Smith was on his feet, holding his shattered rifle, and his eyes were those of a whipped dog-brown and sobbing and water-rimmed.

"I learned my lesson," he said.

Funeral had his voice and he said, "Almost too late for me," and he added, "An old army trick, and you fell for it."

"What happened to . . . Gardner?"

Funeral gestured toward the rocks there on the side of Rising Butte. "Up there," he said. He called, "Who is there?"

First, a woman came out of the rocks, and Funeral said, "Millie Wetherford," but she did not carry a rifle, and he knew that a rifle had killed Clint Gardner. The sharp *spang* of the report had told him that. A pistol talked with harsh throatiness; a rifle spat in feminine deadliness.

Then another figure came out of the boulders and Funeral O'Neill said, "Ed Burnett," and Ed Burnett, raising his rifle, shouted down at them.

"Millie doubled back, and she untied me."

Within a week, the whole matter was

settled, for once and for all. For the traveling judge was due in town and he called this as his first case. Funeral O'Neill had been rather busy. He had had lots of undertaking work to do, and he had also had to embalm Williams, who died the day after being shot by Ed Burnett.

The Circle S cowpunchers had fled the country, for with their boss dead there was nothing to hold them on this range. Therefore the judge declared the big ranch a ward of the county, disposition of the assets to be determined by a jury of six men, and Ringbone Smith and Funeral O'Neill were appointed as members of this body, for Gardner apparently had no heirs – or, if he had heirs, nobody knew where they were located.

Henderson, recovering from his wound, turned state's evidence, and he drew ten years at the penitentiary, with no chance for parole. He told about Gardner sending Colt Hagen over to attempt to kill Ed Burnett.

The judge pounded with his gavel. "That then clears Mr. Burnett of a murder charge."

"How about his breaking out of jail?" Sheriff Dunlap demanded.

The judge hammered again with his gavel. "Court is adjourned," he intoned. He and Funeral and Ringbone had had a long talk in private unknown to Sheriff Dunlap and there he had heard the whole story – how Funeral had smuggled Ed a gun, and he had admitted Funeral had done the right thing.

Sheriff Dunlap hurriedly said, "But, Your Honor, please. This man broke jail – slugged my deputy – "

"I repeat it only once more," the judge said sternly. "This court is adjourned, Sheriff Dunlap."

Conflicting emotions tugged at the sheriffs face. He looked at the dead pan face of Funeral O'Neill and then at the somber face of Ringbone Smith. Then he shrugged and moved away without another word.

He did not see the judge wink at Funeral.

The judge cleared his throat. "Now, I have a pleasant duty to perform. It calls for two people to come forward." He peered at a paper. on his desk. "One person is Millie Wetherford, the other is Mister Ed Burnett."

Millie whispered to Funeral O'Neill. "I want you to stand up with Ed, Mister O'Neill."

"With pleasure, Millie."

Ringbone Smith moved in with, "I'm givin' the bride away. Now, honey, Millie, take hold of my arm, please.

Old Slim Jenson came forward, squeeze-box wheezing out a wedding march. Ringbone patted Millie's hand resting on his arm. Ed Burnett came forward, smiling happily.

Funeral moved in beside Ed. "Well, here we go," said Funeral O'Neill.

Other titles in the Linford Western Library:

TOP HAND
Wade Everett

The Broken T was big. But no ranch is big enough to let a man hide from himself.

GUN WOLVES OF LOBO BASIN
Lee Floren

The Feud was a blood debt. When Smoke Talbot found the outlaws who gunned down his folks he aimed to nail their hide to the barn door.

SHOTGUN SHARKEY
Marshall Grover

The westbound coach carrying the indomitable Larry and Stretch headed for a shooting showdown.

FIGHTING RAMROD
Charles N. Heckelmann

Most men would have cut their losses, but Frazer counted the bullets in his guns and said he'd soak the range in blood before he'd give up another inch of what was his.

LONE GUN
Eric Allen

Smoke Blackbird had been away too long. The Lequires had seized the Blackbird farm, forcing the Indians and settlers off, and no one seemed willing to fight! He had to fight alone.

THE THIRD RIDER
Barry Cord

Mel Rawlins wasn't going to let anything stand in his way. His father was murdered, his two brothers gone. Now Mel rode for vengeance.

ARIZONA DRIFTERS
W. C. Tuttle

When drifting Dutton and Lonnie Steelman decide to become partners they find that they have a common enemy in the formidable Thurston brothers.

TOMBSTONE
Matt Braun

Wells Fargo paid Luke Starbuck to outgun the silver-thieving stagecoach gang at Tombstone. Before long Luke can see the only thing bearing fruit in this eldorado will be the gallows tree.

HIGH BORDER RIDERS
Lee Floren

Buckshot McKee and Tortilla Joe cut the trail of a border tough who was running Mexican beef into Texas. They stopped the smuggler in his tracks.

BRETT RANDALL, GAMBLER
E. B. Mann

Larry Day had the choice of running away from the law or of assuming a dead man's place. No matter what he decided he was bound to end up dead.

THE GUNSHARP
William R. Cox

The Eggerleys weren't very smart. They trained their sights on Will Carney and Arizona's biggest blood bath began.

THE DEPUTY OF SAN RIANO
Lawrence A. Keating and Al. P. Nelson

When a man fell dead from his horse, Ed Grant was spotted riding away from the scene. The deputy sheriff rode out after him and came up against everything from gunfire to dynamite.

and careless about who he gunned down . . .